Diana's To-Do List.

Summer:

1. Take the twins to the beach.

2. Start a diet.

3. Finish my book.

Labor Day:

1. Look for Mr. Right.

2. Fall in love.

3. Get married—and pregnant.

Dear Reader,

When I was little girl, I spent a lot of time at my grandma El's house in New Jersey. She'd greet me at her sweet little cottage on Eckhardt Terrace with freshly baked cookies and—

Oops! That's somebody else's grandma! My grandma El did the mambo, wore Tigress perfume and had a seventy-something-year-old lover who liked to crawl across the kitchen floor to kiss her feet while she washed dishes.

But that's not what I wanted to tell you about. I loved going to Grandma El's house because I got to spend time with the family next door. The Converys were a large, loving family of five kids, two parents and one semi-adopted curly-haired kid from Queens (me!). I'm an only child, and those summers with the Convery kids gave me a taste of how it would be to have brothers and sisters.

I loved all the Converys, but my favorites were the twins, Mary Ann and Gerarda. I could tell them apart, and it amazed me that few others could. I trailed them around like a puppy dog and delighted in watching them play twin jokes.

Thanks to them I've always had a soft spot for twins, and when I sat down to write *Mother Knows Best* I decided it would be great fun to re-create the Convery twins in the guise of Kath and Jenny. I decided it would be more fun to set them loose on Diana Travis. Diana is single and childless and she hasn't a clue. She loves her nieces, but she doesn't know the first thing about caring for toddlers or about family life. Enter Greg Stewart, who's about to give her a crash course in life and love.

Family life is mysterious, glorious, fraught with peril and rich with rewards if you just know where to look. I hope you enjoy this story of family life called *Mother Knows Best.*

With great affection,

Barbara Bretton

BARBARA BRETTON

Mother Knows Best

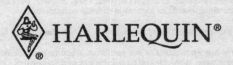

HARLEQUIN®

TORONTO • NEW YORK • LONDON
AMSTERDAM • PARIS • SYDNEY • HAMBURG
STOCKHOLM • ATHENS • TOKYO • MILAN • MADRID
PRAGUE • WARSAW • BUDAPEST • AUCKLAND

ISBN-13: 978-0-373-36108-3
ISBN-10:   0-373-36108-4

MOTHER KNOWS BEST

www.eHarlequin.com

Printed in U.S.A.

BARBARA BRETTON

Barbara Bretton is a *USA TODAY* bestselling, award-winning author of more than forty novels. Barbara has written for the Harlequin American Romance, Harlequin Historical and Harlequin Intrigue lines, as well as for MIRA Books, Pocket Books, Crown Books and Berkley Books.

Barbara, a New Jersey resident, loves to spend as much time as possible in Maine with her husband, walking the rocky beaches and dreaming up plots for upcoming books. If she could walk and knit and read at the same time, her life would be just about perfect.

For Barbara and Rosemary,
those two happy campers

For Deby, who sent me back to camp a second time
and
For my father, who doesn't have
to go to camp anymore.

Happy retirement, Pop!

Chapter One

"Upset? Why should I be upset?" Diana Travis tossed the last suitcase into the back of her rented station wagon, then turned to face her sister. "The fact that I have ten pounds to lose, a book deadline, and an ex-husband who's marrying a twenty-two-year-old, pregnant cheerleader is nothing to get upset about."

"I know what you're doing," Paula Bradley said, shaking an index finger at Diana. "You're trying to make me feel guilty. I'm not to blame for the weight, the book or Jack's indiscretion, but I am giving you a month gratis in the glitzy Hamptons. I have absolutely nothing to feel guilty about. What I meant was, I think you're upset about having the girls and Boris with you."

"Wrong again, sister dear." Diana glanced fondly at her twin nieces, Kath and Jenny. "The girls are the least of my worries. Taking care of children is easy, if you're organized."

Paula made an unpleasant face. "Try being organized in the face of double diaper rash, double tantrums, and double doses of 'me first.' Not even you, Ms. Happy Homemaker, can cope with all of that and stay sane."

"Taking care of the girls is a piece of cake. What I want to know is, who on earth is Boris?"

"A mynah bird," Paula mumbled, eyes darting away from Diana. "He goes with the house."

"A mynah bird? Forget it," Diana said, appalled. "I have a cat."

"Ignatius isn't a cat. He's his own zip code."

"In my present condition I don't appreciate fat jokes. Besides, I don't think Ignatius would make a good bunk mate for a mynah bird."

"Don't worry," said Paula, shaking her head ruefully "Boris doesn't bunk with anybody. He has his own room."

Diana groaned and leaned against the fender of the Cutlass "I knew I hated the Hamptons. Next thing, you'll tell me Boris has a Rolls-Royce and his own driver."

"Laurence is eccentric," Paula said, "but he isn't crazy He just happens to be very fond of Boris."

Laurence McClellan was New York City's premier drama critic. Paula's husband Art handled Laurence's legal matters and when Paula heard McClellan planned to rent out Gull Cottage for the summer, she twisted her husband's arm into reserving the month of July for them.

"If he's so fond of Boris, why didn't he take the bird with him to Europe?"

"Quarantine laws," said Paula.

"Then I'll arrange for Boris to spend the month with a bird sitter."

"You don't understand, Diana. You *are* the bird sitter. That was part of the deal Art made. How else do you think we could afford a place like Gull Cottage?"

Both extortion and embezzlement crossed Diana's mind, but she kept her own counsel. "Okay, you have me cornered. I'm baby-sitting a bird this month. What do I do for him?"

At least Paula had the decency to look sheepish in her triumph, Diana thought.

"It's really very simple. I have a list of things he eats, the music he likes—"

"Van Halen is out, and if that bird thinks he's listening to Lionel Richie, I'll—"

"—and his schedule. I tucked it in with the girls' health records."

"Are you sure you and Art really have a chance to go to Monte Carlo, and this isn't a complicated plan to escape baby-sitting a mynah bird?"

"Would I have spent so much on the beaded strapless, if I were hiding out in the Holiday Inn off the expressway?"

"I just wish you'd told me about Boris before."

"Are you crazy? Do you think I'd give you a chance to figure a way out of this arrangement? Besides, I know you. You'll have that bird on a schedule before the first sunset."

Bringing order to other people's lives was what Diana did for a living. As the woman behind "Mother" in "Mother Knows Best," a nationally syndicated column of household hints and sage advice that had swept the country and turned her own life upside down, Diana was riding the current of success.

Her mother, Peggy, had written the column for twenty years with modest success, and when she married an Irish nobleman and retired to his castle near Dublin, she handed over the column to Diana, who'd been struggling along, writing confession stories and how-to-change-your-own spark plug articles—and praying for her big break.

Fortunately Diana recognized her big break when she saw it. Within three months, she had turned the column into a combination of "Dr. Ruth" and "Heloise's Helpful Hints," and zoomed straight to the top.

"Mother" could take grape juice stains out of an antique lace wedding gown. She could eliminate diaper rash with a wave of her hand. Canine bad breath, the mysteries of sock-eating clothes dryers and why long-stemmed roses died within twenty-four hours, while dandelions lived forever— "Mother" had the answers, and she delivered them five times a week and twice on Sunday, right to the front door-steps of over sixty million American families, desperate to bring order to their chaotic households.

The only problem was, the woman behind "Mother" didn't have a household to call her own. Divorce had followed hard on the heels of her big success, and Diana had found herself going from one short-term rental apartment to another, trying on different towns the way her mother tried on hats. Three months ago, on the eve of her thirty-fifth birthday, she'd been opening a can of seafood buffet for Ignatius, when she'd caught a glimpse of her reflection in the door of her microwave oven and shuddered.

Somewhere along the way she'd made a wrong turn, but for the life of her she couldn't figure out where. Paula, the flightier of the two sisters, had ended up with a loving husband, two beautiful daughters and a big Colonial house in the hills of New Jersey.

Instead of a handsome husband, Diana had an overweight, Abyssinian cat with poor table manners. Instead of warm and loving dinnertime conversation, she had Vanna and *Wheel of Fortune*. The house of her dreams existed solely in black-and-white in her daily newspaper column.

What had happened to her rose-covered cottage with central air conditioning and an attached garage? Where were her 3.2 children? Suddenly it seemed that her biological clock was ticking louder than Big Ben.

Ignatius, tethered by a leather leash, howled his dismay at being treated like a common house cat. Ignatius disliked everything and everybody except food and Diana, in that order. There was nothing like a spoiled Abyssinian to push all thought of biological imperatives from a woman's mind and bring her back to the matter at hand.

It took a good half hour to get the twins into their car seats and another fifteen minutes to reassure her sister that yes, Diana would obey all speed limits, lock the doors at night, and have Paula's Monte Carlo address and phone number tattooed on her forehead for future reference.

"Why don't you go to East Hampton, and I'll go to the Riviera?" Diana suggested. "That's the fifth time you've told me Kath hates peaches and Jenny loves grapes."

Paula's tone was huffy. "You're not a mother. I wouldn't expect you to understand."

"Congratulations. You've now taken separation anxiety to

Olympic levels. I'm your older sister, remember? I'm the one who taught you how to burp and diaper these two monsters. I think I can be trusted with them.''

''Burping and diapering are a far cry from full-time mothering.''

''I know. That's one of the reasons I'm looking forward to spending a month with them. I need the practice.''

Her sister's eyes widened. ''You're not—?''

''No, I'm not.'' Diana flashed a saucy grin. ''At least, not yet.''

Paula grabbed Diana by the lace collar of her Laura Ashley dress. ''I want his name, rank and serial number.''

''I'll tell you everything after Labor Day.''

''Now,'' said Paula. ''You may be older, but I'm tougher.''

''There's nothing to tell.''

''I don't believe you.''

''Honest, Paula. There hasn't been a man within one hundred yards since Jack and I split. I'm going to use this month in the Hamptons as basic training.''

''Basic training?'' Paula glanced at her daughters with a worried expression on her face. ''What are you planning to do, invade Afghanistan?''

''Nothing that easy,'' said Diana, gently disengaging herself from her sister's grip. ''I intend to starve, torture and perm myself into shape while I'm out there, finish my book, then fling myself body and soul into the marriage market, beginning Labor Day.''

Paula reached for the strap on Kath's car seat. ''Come on, girls, your Aunt Diana has lost what remained of her mind.'' She cast a skeptical look at Diana. ''Do you really think these things can be planned out in your daybook?''

''You're the one who's always telling me it's time to think about settling down again.''

''Sure, blame me for this sudden insanity.''

''You must admit you've played matchmaker more than once this year.''

"Can you blame me? I'm getting worried about you, flitting from apartment to apartment like a gypsy. Visiting family, staying with friends—helping everyone else cope with ring around the collar and diaper rash and yellow, waxy buildup, while that damned cat is turning into Orson Welles right before your eyes."

"I agree," Diana said calmly. "I'm not getting any younger. It's time I thought about marrying again and starting a family."

"It may not be that easy."

"One word about having a better chance of being kidnapped by terrorists, and I'll force you to spend a month with Boris." She met her sister's eyes. "Don't look so worried; I have my strategy all worked out."

"Strategy? This sounds like a combination of *Rambo* and *How to Marry a Millionaire*," Paula said. "I think you're more like Dad than Dad was."

"I'll take that as a compliment." Their father Vernon had been nicknamed "The General" for his notorious predilection for timetables, deadlines and schedules that had kept his household operating with the precision of a Swiss watch. "Such a shame you took after Mother. You might have been on time for your own wedding."

"Art has had the decency to forget that incident, Diana. I would think my own sister could do the same."

"Look, Paula," Diana said, patting her sister on the arm, "I'm too old and too jaded to expect Prince Charming is about to look me up in the phone book and swoop over to get me in his white Jaguar."

"How could he, when you change your address every six weeks?"

"Be that as it may, I've studied all the books on the subject, spoken to all the experts, and once summer's over, I intend to devote myself full-time to finding a husband and—not incidentally—a father for my child."

Paula shivered. "I hate when you talk like that. You sound so…"

"Practical?"

"Calculating."

"Thank you again. This is important to me, and I think it deserves my full consideration."

"Has it occurred to you that this plan of yours may fail?"

Diana shook her head. "Never. Believe me, nothing can go wrong. After Labor Day I intend to find a husband, and by this time next year, you'll be planning my baby shower."

Paula's look of disbelief was hardly flattering. "You realize there are other ways to have a child these days, don't you, Di? You don't necessarily have to throw yourself headlong into marriage. If your clock is ticking that fast, maybe you should have a talk with Dr. Stein and—"

"I don't want to talk with Dr. Stein. All I want is to meet a wonderful man, fall madly in love, then have his baby. Is that so much to ask?"

"And you probably expect your career to continue zooming right along, don't you?"

"Motherhood doesn't affect the brain cells, does it?"

"Jury's out. I'll let you know when the twins hit puberty." Paula shot her the kind of sharp look that used to work when they were teenagers. "Your problem is, you want it all."

"Doesn't everyone?"

"Of course, but you believe you'll actually get it. If you weren't my sister, I think I'd hate you."

"If I weren't your sister, we wouldn't be standing here, having this ridiculous conversation, while the girls drool all over their car seats."

Paula's pretty face was awash with earnest concern. "You're unrealistic, Di. It's all about compromise, whether you like it or not. Nobody has it all, and you're crazy if you believe you'll be any different."

"I know I'll be different," said Diana as she coerced a hissing Ignatius into his cat carrier and placed it on the front passenger seat. "It's simply a matter of good planning."

"Haven't you heard?" asked Paula, a wry tone in her voice. "The best part of life is the part you don't plan."

"Then I'm out of luck, because I have my life planned right up to the day I start collecting social security."

Paula shuddered. "How depressing. I couldn't exist without the element of surprise."

"I know," said Diana. "You were surprised to find yourself engaged to Art. You were surprised to find yourself married to Art. And you were surprised to find yourself the mother of twins. So far, you're batting a thousand." How her sister could manage to seem so happy in the middle of utter chaos was beyond Diana. Paula seemed to float on a current of total bewilderment that boggled the mind.

Diana didn't believe in chaos; she believed in schedules and lists, in prioritizing and compartmentalizing all the minutiae of life, and right now she was determined to care for her nieces, meet her book deadline, get a tan and lose ten pounds.

As "Mother" always said, you could even eat an elephant, if you did it one bite at a time.

"You'll call me the minute you get to the house," Paula said as she kissed her daughters one last time and made certain their seat belts were securely fastened over their car seats. "Mrs. Geller will meet you in front around six, to give you the keys and explain how everything works."

"I hope she'll be able to explain this mynah bird I'm saddled with."

"Look," said Paula, looking wonderfully guilty, "Art and I didn't know about Boris until last night. There's nothing wrong with this deal, Diana, honestly. It's a gorgeous, modern house with a view of the ocean to die for and a price you wouldn't believe. We'd be going there ourselves, if this business trip hadn't popped up."

"Monte Carlo in July. Some people will do anything to escape a New Jersey summer."

"I knew you'd understand." Paula kissed her on the cheek and shooed her into the station wagon. She took another longing glance at her daughters, who were fussing in the back seat. "They look unhappy. Maybe they need changing."

Diana sighed loudly. "They were just changed ten minutes ago, Paula. They're fine."

"You'll remember to child-proof the beach house the way I told you?"

"I did three columns on it last month. Unless these kids are junior safecrackers, they don't stand a chance at getting into trouble."

"Writing a column and actually doing it are two different things, Di," her sister pointed out gently. "It may not be all you think."

Diana slid behind the wheel, turned the key, and the engine rumbled to life. "What better way for me to discover the joys and pitfalls of motherhood than by living the experience? It will be good practice for the real thing."

"There is no practice for the real thing. It's strictly baptism by fire."

Diana glanced at her watch. "If I'm going to make it to the Hamptons before six, I'd better hit the road."

"You're certain you know how to get there?" Paula asked. "Maybe you should have flown from Newark Airport to Islip, and rented a car on the Island."

Diana gestured toward the computer-generated map taped to the dashboard. "Courtesy of IBM and Rand McNally. I couldn't get lost if I wanted to."

"The key to everything is the Riverhead exit," Paula persisted. "Make sure you head toward the south fork, not the north."

"Stop worrying," said Diana, irked by her sister's apparent lack of faith. "Besides, I have a fantastic sense of direction. I made a trip through the jungles of Peru. How difficult can Long Island be?"

"It's not the terrain that worries me," said her sister. "It's your traveling companions. They can be extremely disconcerting."

"Don't worry. The girls and I have an understanding. I

don't feed them spinach, and they don't wake me up before
8:00 a.m.'' She put the car into Reverse and began to roll
down the driveway. ''Believe me, Paula, everything's under
control.''

Chapter Two

"Pee-pee."

"I'm hearing things." Diana carefully maneuvered the station wagon through a puddle deep enough to sink a tank. "You cannot possibly need the bathroom again."

"Pee-pee."

She glanced into the rearview mirror at the innocent, chocolate-stained faces of her nieces. "Tell me you're kidding, girls. Tell me this is your idea of a good joke."

Kath shook her head, her blond curls bobbing around her ears with the motion. "Now!"

Jenny looked at her mirror image, then at Diana. "Now," the child repeated at a decibel level reserved for B-52 bombers. "Right now!"

If Diana had learned anything these last three hours, she'd learned that two-year-olds never joked about chocolate, puppy dogs or bathrooms; if she intended to salvage the interior of the rented station wagon from further assault, she needed to find a rest room, pronto.

Not that there were any around, mind you. The road was tree-lined and lovely, peppered with farms and vineyards and an occasional house or two, but the signs of civilization she'd expected were conspicuously absent.

Why on earth had she thought getting off the Long Island Expressway was such a brilliant idea? When the air-conditioning conked out about five miles before Riverhead, escaping the knot of overheated cars had seemed inspired thinking. But now even the bumper-to-bumper traffic that had brought the highway to a virtual standstill from the New York City line all the way out to Mastic Beach seemed preferable to being lost in the middle of nowhere. Didn't these people believe in road signs?

Next to her, Ignatius meowed pitifully and extended one elegant paw through the bars of his cat carrier.

"I know, friend," Diana said, "but you wouldn't bail out on me after all these years, would you?"

Ignatius let loose a horrendous yowl that set the twins giggling in the back seat.

"What good are you, anyway?" Diana grumbled affectionately. "I've read those stories about cats who find their way across ten states, the Rocky Mountains and three time zones, looking for their beloved master." She tapped his extended paw lightly with a finger and grinned at his annoyed hiss. "The least you could do is find East Hampton for me."

After all, it wasn't as though Long Island was the size of Texas. It was a nice, manageable stretch of land bounded on all sides by bodies of water, one of which—the Atlantic Ocean—she was certain to run into any moment.

"Pee-pee!" the girls chorused.

"I'm doing my best," she said, praying Pampers and Scotchgard lived up to all the wonderful things she'd written about them. Did collision insurance cover reupholstering the back seat?

Kath burst into tears, and after a beat, Jenny followed suit. The uproar apparently got under Ignatius's royal skin, and he upped the volume on his high-pitched howling.

"Everything's under control," Diana said, trying to convince herself. "There's no reason on earth to get upset."

This was America, land of the Big Mac and the Whopper and sparkling-clean rest rooms. Any moment she'd round a bend and there, glittering in the late-afternoon sun, would be the golden arches that made every citizen's heart beat faster.

Unfortunately the only thing around each bend in this road

was another bend. Didn't people on the east end of Long
Island eat hamburgers? This had to be the one strip of American roadway without a fast-food joint on the horizon.

Now Diana had always considered trendy summer resorts
with the kind of scorn she reserved for sushi bars and singles'
weekends, but she'd never once imagined they lacked the
normal creature comforts the rest of the population enjoyed.
Good grief, she hadn't even seen a gas station in more miles
than she dared count, and the needle on the gauge was moving inexorably toward E.

The din inside the station wagon grew unbearable and so,
she assumed, did the girls' discomfort. Paula's twenty-minute
discourse on toilet training came back to haunt her. "They'll
tell you what they need," her sister had said that morning.
"Follow their lead, and you won't have any trouble."

"I'd love to follow their lead," Diana muttered now in
desperation, "if I could only find a place."

Her sister's approach to toilet training had a great deal to
do with clean bathrooms, booster seats and a certain degree
of privacy. Diana didn't dare imagine what traumas she
would be inflicting on the twins if she pulled over to the side
of the road and tried to introduce them to the wonders to be
found behind a hedge of rhododendrons.

"Mother," her alter ego, would know what to do.
"Mother Knows Best" had a thousand and one answers for
mildewed shower curtains, flat soda pop and lipstick on the
collar. That resourceful woman would advise Diana to pull
right into someone's driveway, tap on the door, and prevail
upon the mercy inherent in most people when faced with two
adorable, blond toddlers and one not-so-adorable, blond adult
who was about to go over the edge.

Three driveways.

Three houses.

Three strikes and you're out.

Diana got back into the car, rested her forehead against
the steering wheel, and wished she could click her white
sandals together three times and find herself back in her sis-

ter's Colonial house with the central air conditioning and two
and a half bathrooms.

"Who's kidding whom?" she said out loud. At this point
she'd settle for just the half.

"Somethin' wrong, lady?"

Diana jumped at the sound of a man's voice by her open
window.

"Those kids of yours are making a real racket."

Was there a law about noise in the Hamptons? she wondered but, discretion being the better part of valor, didn't ask.
Eight-feet-tall policemen rarely appreciated attempts at sar-
casm.

"I'm sorry," she managed, barely able to disguise the
edge in her voice. "We're having a minor crisis."

"Anything I can help with?"

"Only if you can tell me where I can find the nearest rest
room."

"Pee-pee!" screamed the girls from the back seat.

The policeman stuck his head inside the open window and
glanced at the two squalling toddlers. "Gotta go? Is that the
problem?"

What was wrong with the man? Did he need an affidavit
scribbled on a soggy Pampers as proof?

"They need a bathroom," she said abruptly. "Any
ideas?"

He pointed toward a huge azalea along some fencing.
"Plenty of privacy back there."

She looked closely. "And plenty of poison ivy, too. There
must be a McDonald's somewhere close by."

"None that I can think of."

"Burger King?"

He shook his head.

"White Castle?"

He made a face.

"Pizzeria? Chinese restaurant? Gas station? *Your* house?"
she asked in desperation.

"There's the Sweet Hollow General Store up ahead about

a mile." He looked in again at the wailing twins and the screeching cat. "Think they can hold out?"

"We've made it this far. I'm sure we can make it another mile." She started the engine. "You're sure they have bathrooms?"

"Positive." He narrowed his eyes and made no move to allow her to leave. "They seem to be yelling pretty good back there. Anything wrong I should know about?"

She did her best to maintain her temper. "There's nothing wrong that a rest room couldn't cure." She put the car into drive. "If there's nothing else..."

Finally he moved away from the window.

"I appreciate your help," she offered. "I'm glad to discover the Hamptons' finest are so efficient."

What an odd look that policeman gave her, as she moved back into the traffic. She'd almost swear he made a note of her license plate number, although it was hard to believe any known criminals made a habit of traveling with a pair of toddlers and one neurotic cat.

Diana cast a glance into her rearview mirror and shuddered at the pitiful sight that looked back at her. It was a miracle the policeman hadn't arrested her on the spot for vagrancy. Her dark blond curls, which had once been arranged in a casual upsweep, were tumbling about her shoulders in a mass of frosted frizz. Her hazel eyes were wide and desperate and her careful makeup had dissolved along with her belief that two toddlers were as easy as one. She didn't dare wonder why on earth she'd chosen to wear her favorite dry-clean-only Laura Ashley dress; maybe she'd get a column inch on removing apple juice and chocolate kisses from hand-crocheted lace.

She cringed at the thought of all those cheerful how-to tips she dispensed about maintaining "twenty-four-hour beauty on a five-minute investment." Why she hadn't been lynched by a mob of new mothers was a testament to the sense of humor of the American woman.

A half mile up the road, the Sweet Hollow General Store

appeared, just as the policeman had promised. A small, one-story building, it stood some thirty feet off the road, its weathered, red clapboard siding giving evidence to the number of years it had braved the sun and salt air. The palace at Versailles couldn't have been a more welcome sight.

She turned the wheel sharply right, and the wagon's tires kicked up a spray of gravel that pinged off the fenders and windshield. The only other car in sight was a black Corvette of uncertain vintage that gleamed bright in the orange sun of late afternoon. How nice to know that in the land of Rolls-Royces and Mercedes Benzes, there was still someone around who believed in buying American.

Getting the girls out of their car seats turned out to be more difficult than getting them into them had been—due in no small measure to the fact that Diana was utterly alone this time around. Their steady crying, punctuated with frequent hiccups, had her nerves jangling as if she were hooked up to an IV of straight caffeine.

Regular rules of mathematics obviously didn't matter when it came to children, because it had taken her less than a full afternoon to realize that one plus one equaled a great deal more than two, when the objects in question were twin girls.

Sweat rolled down her forehead and into her eyes, and she felt a stream of perspiration forming between her breasts as she struggled with the snaps and buckles on the car seats. She was certain she hadn't looked this terrible since the time she had her wisdom teeth pulled.

Finally she unhooked them both and set them down on the sandy ground next to her, then released Ignatius from his cat carrier, so he could escape the deadly heat of the steaming car. Diana looped his leash around her wrist, scooped up her nieces into her arms, then took off at a clip toward the front door of this oasis in the middle of the wilderness.

Juggling the girls awkwardly, she was about to reach for the doorknob, when she saw the big, red-and-white sign that contained the most unwelcome word in the English language printed neatly across it.

"CLOSED," Kath and Jenny chirped in unison.

"Thank you, *Sesame Street*," Diana said. The store simply couldn't be closed. The vintage Corvette in the parking lot had to belong to somebody.

She knocked on the door with her elbow, waited a second, then knocked again. The scratchy sound of a baseball broadcast filtered out to where she stood on the front step. Desperate times called for desperate measures, etiquette be damned, she tried the doorknob—and to her infinite relief, the door swung open.

The inside of the store was blessedly cool and dimly lighted, and smelled of cedar and cinnamon. Stacks of bright quilts filled a long line of shelves, and copper pots hung from wrought iron hooks overhead. Huge, wooden barrels piled high with penny candy lined the far wall, and if she didn't know better, she would have imagined she'd stepped back into another century, but of course, they didn't have Phil Rizzuto and the New York Yankees in any century but this one.

"Hello! Is anybody here?" The girls wriggled with unmistakable urgency, and Diana pulled a reluctant Ignatius along with her toward the rear of the store.

"Please, if there's anybody around, I desperately need—"

"A bathroom."

The timbre of the man's voice was deep and rich. Diana spun around, to discover that the resonant voice was only the least of his assets. For the first time, she understood the meaning of "tall, dark, and handsome."

"Are you psychic?" she asked. Or just gorgeous?

"Observant." His lopsided grin made his movie-star good looks a shade more human. "In fact, it may be too late."

"Don't say that," she moaned, suddenly aware of the soggy feel of the girls' bottoms. "I forgot to bring the Pampers in with me."

"No problem." He gestured toward a partially opened door near the rear counter. "You get started, and I'll get the diapers for you." There really was no justice in this world;

he not only had a dimple in his left cheek, he was agreeable, as well.

"I'm the red station wagon." *Like he'll think you showed up in a sleek little Corvette.* "The car is open and the box is in the back. You don't know how much I appreciate this—" Ignatius suddenly leaped forward, hissing madly at the sight of a caged parakeet, and Diana struggled to pull him back, hang onto the girls and keep her balance, all at the same time.

"Give me the cat." The dark-haired man unwrapped the leash from around her wrist and gestured to Ignatius who, to Diana's astonishment, sidled over immediately.

Smart cat, Iggy. He wouldn't have to ask me twice, either.

"Abyssinian. About eleven years old."

Her mouth dropped open. "You're amazing. Most people think he's a fat, bald alley cat."

"I didn't say he wasn't fat." The man gestured toward the girls, who by now were howling at full volume. "If you don't get them into the bathroom, you'll have an even bigger problem. I'll get the diapers."

The heat, that was what it was. The heat had gotten inside her brain cells and altered her normal thought patterns. Why, if he hadn't ordered her into the bathroom with the twins, she might have stood there for the next decade or two staring up at him like a love-struck calf.

He disappeared out the front door, and Diana finally regained control of her equilibrium. She whisked the twins into the bathroom, where it turned out to be too late for one child and just in time for the other. The room was small but clean, so she put Kath onto the john and sat Jenny down on a bright red towel and removed her soggy diaper.

"I told you pee-pee," the child said, her blue eyes wide.

"I know you did, honey. I just couldn't find a bathroom quick enough."

"Hungry," said Kath from her vantage point above them. "Pizza and bananas."

Diana made a face. "I'm glad you're not a chef. How about pizza and pepperoni instead?"

Jenny's laugh mirrored her twin's. "Pizza and popcorn."

Diana kissed the top of the head. "How about just plain pizza, and we'll have ice cream later?" *Forgive me, Paula. It's been one of those days.* It would be nothing but green salads, milk and lean chicken from tomorrow onward.

"Sounds good to me." Her savior stood in the doorway, carrying two boxes of diapers, one marked Super and the other Extra Super. "Take your pick."

Smiling gratefully, she grabbed the former. "Extra Super are for nighttime."

He arched a dark brow. "Might come in handy for car trips."

"This should do fine. We're almost there." She was about to slide the diaper under Jenny's bottom, when she stopped and looked up at him. "I don't know how to ask you this, but I need the baby wipes."

"In the car?"

"In the car."

Again he disappeared out the door, and again he was back in an instant. Here was easily the most glorious man she'd seen in many a year, and she was discussing baby wipes with him. Was there no justice in this world?

"How old are they?" He leaned against the doorjamb with Ignatius at his feet, and watched as she cleaned up Jenny, then moved on to Kath.

"Two plus." She pushed a lock of hair off her forehead with the back of her arm. Why on earth did he have to stand there and watch her final collapse? Didn't he have anything better to do? "A very difficult age."

"Her arm is stuck in the sleeve."

She extricated the tiny limb. "Thank you."

"I think you dropped the other one's shoe behind the sink."

Sure enough. Jenny's bright red sneaker rested on its side near the cold water pipe.

"Thank you again."

He nodded, arms folded across his broad chest. "You look like you're having a problem. Why don't you let me help?"

Did everyone in the Hamptons have an opinion on child care? There was a limit to how much humiliation she was willing to endure in one twenty-four-hour span. "If you really want to help, you and Ignatius can wait for us out front."

He was gone before she could call back her words.

"Isn't that just wonderful," she mumbled as she buttoned Kath back into her pink romper. "The man saves our lives, and I toss him out of his own bathroom."

She discarded the soiled diaper, washed her hands, then led the girls back out into the store proper, a polite smile plastered on her face.

He was crouching near the front door, scratching Ignatius's round belly. The sight of his long, tanned fingers moving rhythmically across the cat's body did something odd inside her, and she took a deep breath. He was looking down, so she couldn't see his face, but she already knew about the glittering, blue eyes, the cleft chin and the shiny, dark brown hair that would still be thick and wavy even after it had turned silver. His waist was lean and his legs were long, which made his football-player shoulders look even more imposing. He was a man in his prime, radiating good health and vitality—a living, breathing advertisement for Made in America. Casually dressed in faded jeans and a red T-shirt, he managed to look better than most men did in tuxedos.

"Well," Diana said brightly, painfully aware of her own disarray, "thank you for all your help." She pulled a dollar bill from her pocket and laid it on the counter.

"What's that for?" he asked, rising and handing her the cat's leash.

"The towel. It needs laundering."

"Keep it." He approached her, and instinctively she shrank back. He stood easily a foot above her own five feet, four inches, and radiated such pure, male power that visions of pirates and privateers rose unbidden to her mind.

She pocketed the money. "Thank you again." Still smiling, she led the girls and Ignatius down the front steps and headed across the gravel toward the station wagon with her pirate-savior right behind. She stopped a few feet before the car and wheeled around. "Is there something else?"

He raised his hand, and her car keys glittered in the waning sunlight. "Can't get too far without these."

"I'm not usually like this," she said, accepting the keys from him. "You may find this hard to believe, but I'm normally one of the most well-organized people you'd ever meet."

"You're right." Fortunately, his expression was masked by glare. "I do find it hard to believe. You were having a hell of a time back there. In fact, if those kids didn't look so much like you, I'd swear you'd kidnapped them."

Diana smiled and said nothing. If she launched into an explanation about Paula and Art and the great pre-Labor Day mothering experience, he'd probably call the police and have her put away on grounds of insanity.

"Thank you yet again," she said finally, praying he'd let her slink off into the sunset. "We're just fine. You can finish closing up or whatever it was you're doing."

"All closed up. All I have to do now is leave."

"You don't have to wait around for me. It takes a while to get the girls into their car seats and Ignatius into his carrier."

"Ignatius?"

She shrugged. "It's a long story."

"If I were named Ignatius, I'd leave town."

"Don't give him any ideas."

She opened the door of the station wagon and lifted the girls into the back seat, with him still watching. While they clambered into position, she bent down to grab a besotted Ignatius, only to be greeted with a furious hiss and a display of claws that a Bengal tiger would have been proud of.

The man grinned and swooped Ignatius into his arms. "Where do you want him?"

"You don't really want to know."

"I'll overlook that."

"The cat carrier will do fine."

He had Ignatius safely locked away in an instant, and still he didn't leave.

"Look," Diana said in exasperation, "I appreciate everything you've done for us, but if you have any other ideas, I'm not interested."

"Glad to hear it, because the only thing I *am* interested in is getting out of here."

She followed his gaze. "The Corvette belongs to you?"

He nodded.

"And I'm blocking you in."

He nodded again.

The whole afternoon had been such an exercise in absurdity that—despite the heat and the humidity and the fact that she looked like bloody hell—Diana started to laugh. "You must feel like tossing me into the Atlantic out there, feet first."

His brow furrowed. "The Atlantic?"

What on earth was the matter with him? He'd seemed quite an intelligent man on first acquaintance. "I mean, that *is* the ocean I smell, isn't it?"

His frown deepened. "No, actually it isn't."

"Right. And I don't suppose this is the way to East Hampton either, is it?" He shook his head, and she was sure the theme song from *The Twilight Zone* was blossoming all around them. "Very funny. I probably deserved it. Which Hampton is this: Bridge-, South-, West...?"

"Not even close."

"I don't think I want to hear this." She sagged against the open door of the station wagon, as Paula's warning about the Riverhead exit came back to haunt her. "Don't say it. I've lost my sense of humor. I'll never live this down."

"This is Southold," he said, obviously not a man afraid to bear bad tidings. "And, lady, you've got a *long* way to go."

Chapter Three

"Okay, I know I deserve that," Diana said, looking up at him. "I come barging into your store at closing time with two cranky toddlers in need of a bathroom, and I don't even have the decency to buy a stick of gum. That's against all rules of polite behavior, and I apologize."

"You can apologize all you want to, but it's not going to change a thing."

"This isn't East Hampton?"

"This isn't East Hampton."

"Am I close?" *Please tell me I'm close.*

"Define the term 'close.'"

Diana's stomach lurched. It was even worse than she'd thought. "Am I in the right state?"

"New York." That infernal grin of his reappeared. "The Empire State. Home of Radio City, the New York Yankees, Wall Street, Fifth Aven—"

"Those I can find. It's the Hamptons that are giving me trouble." Maybe they were a figment of some overzealous press agent's imagination, conjured up to bring glamour to the bucolic eastern end of Long Island, and not real at all. "Will you stop looking at me like that? I'm not a human time bomb about to explode."

"Could've fooled me."

"Look," she said, meeting his eyes. "I could spend a great deal of our valuable time telling you that I don't usually look like this or sound like this or act like this, but I doubt if you'd believe a word I had to say, and I don't blame you. Now if you would just point me in the general direction of East Hampton, I'll thank you and be on my way.''

He leaned against the fender of her station wagon. ''Now you've got me curious: how *do* you usually look?''

''Cleaner, and that's just for starters.'' She was dismayed; how dreadful the apple juice and chocolate stains looked on her delicate, garden party dress! The heat inside the car had sent her makeup running down her cheeks, and she could only imagine the tumble her hair was in, because the entire front seat was littered with the tiny pins that had once held her upsweep in place. The fact that he was drop-dead gorgeous, while Diana looked as if she hadn't mastered the first, basic rules about personal grooming suddenly infuriated her. ''I'm sweaty, frazzled, and overstressed, and I think I'd better find East Hampton before I run out of either diapers or patience.''

''I've heard of 'kill the messenger,' but this is ridiculous.'' The tips of his Nikes pressed against the delicate front of her strappy, white sandals. ''It's not my fault you have two kids, no air-conditioning and a lousy sense of direction. The least you can do is be polite.'' He stormed back to his Corvette, gunned the engine, then waited impatiently for Diana to move the station wagon, so he could leave.

All right, be that way. She slid behind the wheel and unfolded her map of Long Island, ignoring the vroom-vroom of the vintage Corvette's mighty engine. It would be dark soon, and she'd be darned if she ended up stranded on some forgotten country lane with two little girls and a spoiled cat for company.

Okay, there was Riverhead, right where Long Island's fishtail split into the north and south forks. Somehow her brilliant decision to venture off the expressway and onto local roads had taken her far afield. The Peconic and Gardiners bays separated north from south, and short of wishing her station wagon would sprout water wings, it seemed she had no choice but to retrace her steps, even though she wasn't entirely sure what those exact steps had been.

Mr. Tall-Dark-and-Handsome popped up at her open window. "Having trouble, or are you meditating?"

"I'm taking a moment to plot my course."

"You should have thought about plotting your course a few hours ago."

"And have been deprived of the pleasure of your company? Perish the thought."

"Look, as far as I'm concerned, you can stay here all night. Just move your station wagon, so I can leave."

In the back seat the girls giggled, as Ignatius loosed another horrendous yowl.

"Is he your alter ego?" the man asked.

Despite her foul mood, Diana softened. "I deserved that, didn't I?"

"Afraid so."

"I don't know what came over me. The minute you said that wasn't the Atlantic Ocean, I turned into Rambo. I apologize."

His answering smile was incendiary. "Apology accepted."

She started the engine. "I'll move out of your way."

His smile widened. "I'd appreciate that."

Diana hazarded a glance in her rearview mirror and shuddered. No wonder he was so anxious to see her leave. She looked like the "Don't" photo in a beauty magazine. With her foot on the brake, she shifted into Reverse. "You're sure that's not the Atlantic Ocean I hear?"

"Positive."

She sighed. "Hope springs eternal, et cetera et cetera." With a glance over her shoulder to make certain the girls were securely strapped into their car seats, she gave him a salute. "Thanks again. Now it's on to East Hampton." *I hope.*

She waited politely for him to step away from the open car window, but he didn't. "You sure you know how to get to Riverhead?" he asked.

"Follow this road back where I came from. According to the map I can't miss it." The level of the girls' crying went up another two decibels. Ignatius, naturally, matched them and more. It was going to be a long and ugly drive.

"According to the map, you couldn't miss East Hampton, either."

"Another crack about my sense of direction, and I'll pull out of here with you as a hood ornament."

He leaned against the car door, and she caught the beguiling scent of soap and sea air. "Why don't you follow me? I'll get you on the yellow brick road to the Hamptons."

Diana wasn't a New Yorker born and bred for nothing. Suspicion was part of her makeup, and she frowned at him. Mass murderers often came in very attractive packages. For all she knew, he'd lured many a hapless female into his quaint general store and used their bodies for compost to fertilize his tomato plants. "That's very kind, but what's in it for you? Why would you want to go out of your way for a stranger?"

"Because I'm starting to think it's the only way I'll ever get out of this damned driveway, that's why." That friendly smile hid a shimmer of solid steel. This was a man used to having his own way. "Besides, I have an office in Amagansett and I—" He stopped himself short. "Do you want help or not?"

"Yes, but—"

"Back out of the driveway, pull off to the side, then follow me."

"This is very kind of you."

"It's not kindness; it's self-preservation. Another hour or two and there'll be a new batch of wet diapers, and this whole thing will start over again."

"And you don't want to be around for it."

"Now you understand."

"I'll back out of the driveway."

"I'd appreciate it."

It took a while, but after a stop at a gas station, they were rolling westward on Route 25A, heading back toward Riverhead. Diana had no trouble understanding why the Island was called Long; the drive seemed endless. Vineyards and farmlands slowly gave way to small shopping centers and other signs of civilization as they neared Riverhead. The black Corvette clung to the narrow roads with an almost jaunty sense of assurance, and Diana knew its owner must have wished he could shift into a higher gear and leave her in the dust. To the man's everlasting credit, he maintained his regal pace, and Diana had no difficulty keeping him in view, even through the vicious glare from the setting sun.

They swung around through Riverhead and onto Montauk Highway, headed east, and Diana breathed a sigh of relief as the sun moved behind her. Ignatius had finally settled down his bulk to take a nap in his much hated cat carrier, and the girls had stopped crying and were singing Mr. Rogers's theme song.

"This isn't so bad," Diana said, switching on the radio. One tiny setback and she'd been ready to throw in the towel. What a wimp! Taking a wrong turn was hardly the end of the world, and she'd been foolish to act as if it was.

"Who's kidding whom?" She stopped at a traffic light, right behind the black Corvette. It wasn't the wrong turn, the extra driving or the soggy diapers that had been her undoing; it was that vision of male pulchritude that had pushed her over the edge. What a perverse sense of humor had the goddess of single women! Diana knew full well that had she been at her fighting weight, flawlessly made up and dressed in her red, strapless sheath, her savior would have been Woody Allen's long-lost twin brother. But add a few extra pounds to her hips, split ends and a chocolate-stained dress, and what did she get? The perfect man. Six feet, four inches of taut muscles, tanned skin and sparkling, blue eyes, calculated to make any woman's pulse accelerate, even if technically she wasn't in the market for romance for another sixty days.

Bad timing, that was what it was. Except for the day she

took over the "Mother Knows Best" column, Diana's timing had always been the pits, and this was no exception. Come Labor Day, her book deadline would be past; she'd be slim and tanned and shorn of her split ends, ready to venture forth and find her perfect mate. By that time she'd be nothing but an anecdote for Mr. Tall-Dark-and-Handsome to relate to his friends. In fact, he probably couldn't wait to get home tonight and tell the wife and kiddies all about the frazzled and frenzied nincompoop who couldn't tell Long Island Sound from the Atlantic Ocean.

Southampton College whizzed by on her left. "What do you think, girls? Can you imagine keeping your nose to the grindstone in a place like this?"

"Hungry," Kath announced. "You said pizza."

"Not much longer, honey. We're almost there."

Southampton turned into Bridgehampton, which turned into Wainscott, and she knew they had to be getting closer. A few minutes later, the man in the black Corvette tapped his brakes, then motioned her to the shoulder on the right, near a crystal-clear pond. She pulled over behind him, he unfolded his length from the sports car and walked over to her.

"This is it," he said, leaning into the open window once again. "East Hampton, last stop."

She looked at the bright red sunset, reflecting off the shimmering surface of the pond, and the poplars and cedars arching over it. "I'm impressed. It's beautiful."

"Where do you go from here?"

She fumbled in the glove compartment and removed a sheet of Paula's heavy vellum notepaper. Her sister's precise handwriting filled the top half of the page with instructions on the care and feeding of twins; a map worthy of Rand McNally filled the bottom. "Diapers...life preservers... *Sesame Street*...there it is. I'm looking for Frigate Alley."

"Frigate Alley?"

"You sound surprised. Is there something I should

know?'' Paula had said Art got quite a deal on the place. Maybe there was a good reason for it. "I know it's only a cottage, but Paula swore it's not a handyman's special.''

"No,'' he said slowly, "I don't think you have to worry about it being a handyman's special.''

"I don't like that smile on your face. What's wrong? Is Gull Cottage haunted or something?''

"It's not haunted, but a ghost might be an improvement.''

"You're making me nervous. Maybe I'll check into a Howard Johnson's instead.''

"In East Hampton? Not very likely.'' He looked at the girls in the back seat, at Ignatius in his carrying case, then back at Diana. "Want me to take you the rest of the way?''

"I think I'll be fine.'' She repeated Paula's directions out loud and he nodded.

"You shouldn't have any more problems.''

"From your mouth to God's ear.'' She extended her right hand. "Thanks for getting us this far. I might have ended up in Rhode Island.''

Her hand disappeared in his large, tanned one. "You won't get an argument from me.''

She waited for him to relax his grip. "We've taken enough of your time.''

"I was heading this way, anyhow.''

"I'm sure you have better things to do.''

"I was only going to go to—''

"Pizza!'' cried the twins in stereo. *"Now!"*

Both Diana and the man laughed, and the mood, such as it was, was broken. He released her hand and moved away from the car.

"Thanks again,'' said Diana.

"No problem,'' said the man.

It wasn't until Diana was two blocks away that she realized she didn't even know his name.

GREGORY STEWART stood next to his Corvette and watched the station wagon, until it disappeared around a curve in the road.

"Gull Cottage," he said out loud, shaking his head. Laurence McClellan's lavish—and highly mortgaged—palace by the sea. Maybe she was a cook or a housekeeper, hired to keep the current tenants happy, or a high-priced baby-sitter for Boris the Bad, if he was in residence at the moment.

Or she could be renting it herself....

He considered the rented station wagon with the two adorable toddlers in the back seat, the fat cat on a leash, and the woman's general air of chaotic charm. Where were the de rigeur golden retriever, the Aprica double baby stroller, and the au pair with the French accent?

Renting Gull Cottage herself?

Not very likely.

Summer renters only attached themselves to other summer renters. They moved eastward after Memorial Day like some strange kind of migratory animal, traveling in packs from the East Side Highway to the Long Island Expressway to the beaches of East Hampton, until it was time for the mass exodus back to Manhattan, come Labor Day.

Same faces; same bodies; same conversation. Add Bain de Soleil and Kahlua and shake well. The only thing that changed was the latitude.

You could keep it.

That dizzy blonde in her chocolate-stained dress was the most interesting woman he'd seen in a long time. With her quirky sense of humor and her sexily disheveled mane of hair, she'd gotten to him quicker than any woman had in longer than he cared to remember.

Hell, he thought, climbing back into his Corvette. What difference did it make, anyway? Those two little girls looked like miniature versions of her. She was probably ten years married, with a husband who'd be driving out in their beat-up Chevy come the weekend, to help her with the work. The only way he'd be seeing her again was if Boris needed his wings clipped, or her fat cat developed a cold.

Which, all things considered, struck Gregory Stewart as a shame.

Chapter Four

"Big!" said Kath, staring out the car window.

"Castle!" said Jenny, her head pressed next to her twin's.

"Gull Cottage?" asked Diana, shell-shocked.

Cottages were cozy and quaint affairs with thatched roofs and picket fences and two bedrooms, at the most. Gull Cottage, on the other hand, had a sharply slanted roof with three chimneys, a curving drive complete with porte cochere, and what appeared to be space enough to sleep the entire population of Liechtenstein, with room to spare.

There had to be some mistake.

She checked the street sign, then looked down at Paula's map. Both said Frigate Alley in bold letters. The name McClellan was painted proudly on the weathered mailbox at the end of the driveway. But why on earth was there a moving van parked under the porte cochere? And a frantic woman standing in the doorway with worry beads dangling from her hands?

Diana eased the car up the gravel driveway and pulled in behind the moving van. Pocketing the car keys, she turned to the girls. "Stay here," she said, offering them each a biscuit. "I'll be right back."

"And then pizza?" Kath asked, ever hopeful.

Diana's stomach rumbled in anticipation. "And then pizza." Goodbye to her diet. It would be a miracle if she didn't dive headfirst into a carton of Häagen-Dazs before the night was over.

Casually she strolled past the moving van and peeked inside. In the gathering dusk it was difficult to distinguish the various shapes inside the truck, but she did manage to pick out enough paintings and sculptures to fill a small museum. An odd feeling grew in the pit of her stomach, and this time she didn't think it was hunger that caused it.

She hurried up the walkway to the front door. "Mrs. Geller?"

The short, dark-haired woman turned, her sensible shoes squeaking against the brick step. "Ms. Travis?"

Diana nodded. She didn't trust her voice.

"Oh, dear!" muttered Mrs. Geller, wringing her worry beads. "I had so hoped I would have this small difficulty ironed out by the time you arrived. We had believed everything had been repo... I mean, appropriated already."

"'Scuse us, ladies. We got a wide load."

Diana jumped out of the way, as two burly moving men carried a stack of crates past them.

"*This* is Gull Cottage?" she asked.

Mrs. Geller's fingers fairly flew over her worry beads. "Cottage is a bit of an understatement, isn't it?"

Diana watched in amazement, as a trio of movers carried out enormous bookcases made of pristine, Swedish oak.

Mrs. Geller draped her beads around her right wrist and pulled a ring of keys from the pocket of her white linen jacket. "Well, here you go, Ms. Travis. Front door, back door, garage. You'll find instructions inside, detailing everything you need to know about the housekeeping service, pool man, security system...." She paused, her brow furrowed. "I can't think of another thing."

"I can," said Diana as another burly mover headed toward the van. "Where is the furniture going?"

"Oh, dear," said Mrs. Geller, as if the question surprised her. "I do hope this won't prove to be a problem."

"Look out!" boomed a brawny mover, who had a rolled-up Persian carpet slung over his shoulder. "Pool table's bringin' up the rear, then the place is all yours."

"Where is everything going?" Diana repeated, ducking out of the way as the rug passed uncomfortably close to her head. "*Why* is everything going?"

Mrs. Geller's fingers did a tap dance on her beads. "Delicate matter, that. It seems our Mr. McClellan made a few bad investments—Broadway is a risky business—and he is attempting to recoup his losses."

Diana arched an eyebrow. "You mean they're repossessing his furniture."

"I was searching for another way to put it." Mrs. Geller turned her worried gaze on Diana. "I have already contacted your brother-in-law and he's accepted another reduction in the monthly rental fee."

"How nice of him," Diana muttered. "Did he also arrange for a fridge and a stove, and the other amenities of twentieth-century life I've grown to know and love?" "Mother" might know how to can tomatoes, make strawberry jam and preserve peaches with the best of them, but she did it with the help of every modern convenience she could get her hands on.

Mrs. Geller brightened. "Not to worry, dear. All major appliances stay with the house. In fact, I believe the master bedroom suite does, as well."

"That's a relief. My two nieces are with me and I—"

"Oh, dear. How old are your nieces?"

"A little over two."

"There aren't any cribs, Ms. Travis. Mr. McClellan's children are adults."

"The girls are out of cribs." Diana hadn't expected Gull Cottage to come equipped with baby furniture, but she had expected a bed or two. "You did say the master suite is intact."

"Oh, yes."

"Complete with a bed?"

Mrs. Geller's plump cheeks turned a becoming shade of

pink. "Oh, yes, my dear. It has a bed and a sunken tub and a breathtaking view."

It could be worse. Diana had no house, no condo, no apartment to call her own, and unless she intended to spend the next four weeks cooped up inside a motel room with the twins and Ignatius, this version of Buckingham Palace, Long Island-style, was her best bet.

"Why not?" she said. "I come from sturdy pioneer stock. I can rough it with the best of them."

Mrs. Geller, bless her humorless heart, nodded and the two women watched as the moving van maneuvered its way around Diana's rented station wagon.

"Well, well," said Mrs. Geller. "That would seem to be that."

A loud squawk rang out from somewhere inside the house.

"They left Boris behind?" Diana asked.

Mrs. Geller's prim mouth pursed. "Messy, dirty creature. That bird has the vocabulary of a—" She caught herself, apparently envisioning her real estate commission disappearing on the next ocean breeze. "He's rather elderly. I shouldn't imagine he requires a great deal of care."

"To be or not to be," Boris boomed. "Only the Shadow knows...."

"He has an impressive set of lungs for an old bird. I'd like to meet him."

Mrs. Geller snapped to attention. "Why don't I give you a tour of the place before I leave?"

"Let me get the twins and Ignatius and we're all yours."

"Ignatius?"

"My cat."

"Oh, dear," said Mrs. Geller. "A cat and Boris...oh, dear."

"Don't worry," said Diana, heading toward the station wagon. "Ignatius is the Orson Welles of the cat kingdom. Boris is in no danger."

Mrs. Geller's look of skepticism changed, the moment she saw the corpulent pet at the end of the leather leash. Ignatius looked for all the world like a deposed potentate in search of a new country to rule.

"I see what you mean," said the real estate agent, her expression brightening. "He is rather..."

"Fat," said Diana, juggling the twins against her hips.

"I was about to say plump."

"He passed plump about three years ago, Mrs. Geller, but it's kind of you to pretend otherwise." *And if I don't start my diet tomorrow morning, Iggy and I will be the Bobbsey Twins.*

They stepped into the foyer. "Welcome to Gull Cottage," said Mrs. Geller.

Even Ignatius stopped in his tracks and stared at the incredible surroundings.

"Are you sure this isn't Wonderland?" Diana breathed, putting the girls down on the immaculate, slate floor. "This looks like Hollywood's idea of the perfect summerhouse."

"Mr. McClellan would be thrilled to hear that analogy. I heard it said he wished to build a cottage worthy of F. Scott Fitzgerald."

"He succeeded."

Mrs. Geller arched one unplucked brow. "One might wish he exhibited more concern toward paying his mortgage than he did toward Olympic-sized swimming pools."

"There's an Olympic-sized swimming pool out back?"

"Heated," said Mrs. Geller. "Long Island Lighting must rub its collective hands together in glee at the very thought."

"Sounds wonderful!" Diana had no intention of letting the girls do more than get their toes wet in the ocean. The thought of currents and undertow and crashing waves was enough to make her blood run cold. It would be great fun, however, to take the girls swimming in the shallow end of the pool, so they could show off the brand-new aquatic skills that Paula had been so insufferably proud of. She looked down at her nieces. "Swimming, girls!" she said brightly. "I'm glad we brought your water wings with us. Doesn't it sound wonderful?"

Their china-blue eyes widened, but neither toddler removed her thumb from her mouth long enough to say a word. They simply stared at the vast expanse of furnitureless foyer with something approaching awe.

"They're tired," Diana said by way of explanation, even though Mrs. Geller seemed more interested in Ignatius than the twins. "It's been a long day."

"Early to bed and early to rise!" Boris called out from somewhere close by. "That's the ticket!"

"Why postpone the inevitable?" asked Mrs. Geller with a sigh. She led the strange parade into the living room, to admire the breathtaking, ocean view from the banks of French doors that Diana sorely wished had child-proof locks.

"Quite remarkable, isn't it?" asked Mrs. Geller.

"Quite," said Diana as they stepped out onto the deck that she would absolutely *never* let the twins play on alone.

And then they entered the solarium, with its soaring ceiling, copper-hooded fireplace and equally breathtaking view. Ignatius spotted Boris first. His tail shot straight up, as he arched his back into an S curve and emitted a hiss that sent shivers up Diana's spine.

"Oh, dear!" exclaimed the ever worried Mrs. Geller. "I don't think Boris will like having a cat stay at Gull Cottage." She made "cat" sound like a four-letter word.

Diana was about to explain Iggy's devotion to sloth, when Boris hopped down to the floor of his cage. The mynah bird tilted his head sideways, fixed Ignatius with a stern look, then said: "Boo!"

In a respectable display of athletic prowess, Iggy leaped a foot into the air, then, paws scrambling, raced for parts unknown.

"I don't believe it. He hasn't moved that fast since the day I had him fixed."

Mrs. Geller turned another shade of pink. "I don't think they like each other."

"Probably not, but I don't foresee any problems. Boris is

safe up there in his cage, and Iggy is intrinsically lazy and earthbound. That wind sprint was an aberration.''

"Two children and a cat.'' Mrs. Geller shook her head. "You must have a great deal of patience, Ms. Travis.''

"Unlimited for animals and children. It's adults I have trouble with.'' She approached the cage, where a wary Boris waited. "You mind your business, Boris, and I'll mind mine. I don't think we'll have any trouble, do you?''

Boris tilted his head as he had with Ignatius, his beady eyes intent upon her. "Come up and see me sometime,'' he invited, a Mae West in feathers, "because when I'm bad, I'm better.''

"Is he X-rated?'' Diana asked, wondering how her sister would react if the twins came back with Joan Rivers's routine down cold.

"I don't believe so. Mostly Shakespeare, Tennessee Williams and a bit of Las Vegas tossed in for good measure.''

"He doesn't sing 'Feelings,' does he?''

Mrs. Geller looked at her blankly but Boris, to her delight, laughed loud and long.

"Boris,'' Diana said solemnly, "I think this is the beginning of a beautiful friendship.''

DAVE REILLY was pacing a hole in the tan carpet, when Greg walked into the back office of the East End Animal Center.

"Anything?'' Greg asked, taking in the other man's haggard face and uncombed hair. Amazing that what looked so sexy on the curly-haired blonde could look plain lousy on his partner.

"Not yet.'' Dave lit a cigarette, grimaced, then stubbed it out in an overflowing ashtray on the desk.

"How many minutes apart?''

"Twenty and counting.''

"So what are you doing talking to me, man? Get your butt out of here.''

"It might be another false alarm,'' Dave said, grabbing his

car keys and fumbling through his pockets for his crumpled pack of cigarettes.

"And it might be the real thing."

"I'll be back if it isn't."

"Stay with Peggy," said Gregory, pushing the younger man toward the door. "You only have one first kid."

"This makes it three nights in a row. It's a hell of a way to build a partnership."

"You'll owe me," said Gregory. "Believe me, it'll even out. Just come back in tomorrow night, if it's a false alarm."

"I really appreciate this." Dave pumped Gregory's hand in such a display of youthful appreciation that the older man could barely suppress his smile. "I'll work weekends and holidays for the next year."

Gregory's smile broke through. "Damn straight you will. I'll be out on my boat before you know it."

"Still going ahead with it?"

"Nothing holding me back, Dave. It's a chance in a life-time."

Dave's expression darkened and he gestured toward the back of the building. "Joey's here."

"This late?"

"He's convinced it'll be tonight."

"Kid's dying for one of Daisy's pups, isn't he?" Greg laughed, then caught himself. "Forget I said it."

Dave nodded and checked his watch. "I'd better motor," he said, heading toward the door. "Maybe we'll name the baby after you."

"Why not?" Gregory said as the door swung closed behind his partner. That was one way for the Stewart name to make it into the next century.

"No regrets, Stewart," he muttered, pouring himself a mug of coffee from the machine atop the battle-scarred desk. Looking back had never figured high in the scheme of things for him; looking forward was the only thing that made sense.

He glanced at the huge calendar hanging on the wall behind the desk. The black Xs were beginning to take over, and he picked up a felt marker and placed another across the square for July 1. There'd been a time when he hadn't believed he'd make it this far; those long dark months of pain and fear were never far away, burning at the edges of his consciousness when he was too tired to turn his mind away from the memories.

Now, after more than four years, it was almost over. Soon he'd be out on the open seas where nothing could get him, where fear couldn't reach him, riding out the last of the wait on a wave of expectation.

He flipped the marker onto the desk, then strolled back to the kennel, to check on Joey and their canine expectant mother.

Bon Jovi blared from a small radio on a far table, and the distinctive aroma of pepperoni pizza wafted through the open door. Gregory stood in the doorway, hands jammed into the pockets of his trousers, and battled with a wave of emotion as violent and dangerous as the Atlantic Ocean crashing not too far away.

Joey wore a Yankee baseball cap pulled low over his forehead and a bright red T-shirt with the words Party Animal scrawled across the chest. Pink patches of scalp showed behind the boy's ears, and the back of his neck was blotchy from the sun. Only the practiced eye would see the pallor beneath the beginning tan, the faint tremor in the fingers stroking the ear of the heavily pregnant dog.

Gregory noticed it all, because he'd been there himself.

Stepping back into the hallway, he took a deep breath, called up his best smile from the old days and strode into the room. "Hey, Joey." He tugged at the bill of the boy's baseball cap. "How's Daisy tonight?"

"Hungry." Joey offered the dog a piece of his pizza.

"Big piece for a small dog."

"She's eating for two, remember?"

Gregory quickly palpated the dog's abdomen and grinned at the boy. "More like eating for five or six. You ask your mom about the puppy yet?"

Joey shrugged his thin shoulders and stared down at the pizza, as if it were a Madonna poster. "No problem."

"You haven't asked her yet," Gregory stated.

"I'll get around to it."

"When? Daisy's going to deliver any time now. You plan on showing up at your back door with a puppy in tow?"

"I kinda figured when she sees the puppy, she couldn't say no."

"A deal's a deal, Marino. You don't ask, you don't get."

If Gregory had his way, the kid could have a score of puppies, a Rolls-Royce and a miracle or two, but he knew Mary Ann Marino—and knew she had more than her share to cope with. Cute as Daisy's pups were bound to be, they just might be enough to push her over the edge.

"Ask her," Gregory repeated, filching a slice of pizza from the white cardboard box on the desk. "What can it hurt?"

"She might say no."

He bit into a circle of pepperoni hot enough to singe his eyelashes. "She might say yes."

"You don't know my mom."

"Short, curly red hair, freckles on her nose?"

Joey's grin was quicksilver; it disappeared almost before it registered itself on Gregory's heart. "Must be her twin."

Gregory scooped up a long string of mozzarella with his fingers and rolled it deftly into his mouth. "Must be."

He'd known Mary Ann since the day he opened the doors of the animal hospital three years ago. She'd been the first and last applicant he'd interviewed for the position of office administrator. Young, ambitious and recently divorced, she'd attacked the job with the ferocity of a small and feisty terrier, and before Gregory knew it, he had both a successful veterinary practice and a friend.

Mary Ann had listened to his ramblings about his broken engagement, fed him tea and sympathy when the uncertainty sometimes got to him, and not least, offered him shelter and a hot meal on those nights when the future seemed particularly dark.

Joey grabbed another slice of pizza. "I wish I had a beer."

Gregory, who'd been thinking the same thing himself, tried hard not to laugh. "Bud Lite?"

Joey's face wrinkled like his mother's did whenever a perfectly coiffed French poodle with pink toenails showed up in the waiting room. "Lite's for kids."

"Pepsi is for kids. Beer's for adults."

"I still want one."

"We can't always get what we want."

Joey was also as pigheaded as his red-haired mother. "I want to see what it tastes like."

"Tastes lousy. You wouldn't like it."

"You have Coors in the fridge in the garage."

Gregory's eyebrows arched. "I do?"

Joey nodded. "From your Memorial Day picnic."

"What else do I have in there?"

"Some green stuff in a Tupperware and a package of bologna."

"You take the bologna. I'll take the beer."

"I'm going to be thirteen soon," Joey said, his brown eyes huge in his narrow face. "That's old enough to try beer."

"Twenty-one is old enough in this state, pal."

Gregory regretted the words, even as he was saying them. Joey's expression lost its sparkle, and he turned into a scared little boy right before Gregory's eyes.

"Got to obey the law," he said offhandedly, as if reality hadn't made a sudden and unwelcome appearance in their midst. "You don't want me carted off to jail for aiding and abetting a minor, do you?"

Joey's sparkle returned. "If it meant I could try beer, I wouldn't mind."

"You're a hell of a pal, Marino," Gregory said, heading toward the garage. "Remember me when the cops show up."

"You're gonna let me have a beer?"

Gregory paused in the open doorway. "A sip. That's it."

"Really?"

"Really."

"Aw-*right!*"

It wasn't much in the scheme of things, but at the moment, a boy's first taste of beer seemed pretty damned important, and Gregory liked the fact that he'd be the man to introduce Joey Marino to the wonders of malt. Kid was bound to hate it—most kids his age would rather have a chocolate milk shake than a beer, and Joey would probably be no exception. But unlike most kids, there was a good chance Joey Marino wouldn't be around when the time came to trade in his sodas for a six-pack.

Chapter Five

"Are you certain you're all right?" Diana peered into Mrs. Geller's eyes. "You gave me quite a scare."

Mrs. Geller gathered her East End aplomb around her shoulders like a cashmere cardigan and managed a shaky smile. "It was those children," she said, glaring down at the twins, who blessed her with cherubic smiles. "Not used to having them underfoot. Quite dangerous."

Diana managed to hold back the observation that the girls hadn't been within ten feet of the real estate agent when she tumbled quite gracefully down the last two steps to the beach. The truth was, Mrs. Geller had been unraveling inch by controlled inch since Diana had arrived at Gull Cottage one hour ago.

"I assure you, the girls and I are quite adaptable," Diana repeated as they strolled back into the solarium, where Ignatius and Boris were engaged in a game of who's-going-to-blink-first. "As long as the utilities work, and the major appliances stay where they are, we'll be fine."

"You're quite the good sport about this, Ms. Travis."

"I can afford to be," Diana said cheerfully. "My brother-in-law is picking up the tab."

"Mr. Bradley is a kind and forgiving man."

Diana's ears pricked up at the sound of possible gossip. "The last tenants," she said, lowering her voice conspiratorially. "How did they handle it? I could just imagine what it must have been like having the furniture snatched right out from under you.''

''The elder Ms. Piper fled before the end of the month, but her niece showed tremendous fortitude and patience.''

Diana thought of the pink papier-màché shark suspended over the dining-room table—or rather, where the dining-room table had once been—the slot machine in one of the upstairs baths, and the Cleopatra's barge of a bed. ''She must have had a sense of humor, as well.''

''Trying circumstances, these,'' said Mrs. Geller, casting Boris a baleful look, as he tossed food pellets at Ignatius and laughed maniacally. ''One wishes to retain one's composure, but one sometimes cannot.''

''What you need is a bracing cup of tea.''

If possible, Mrs. Geller looked even more forlorn. ''No teacups, Ms. Travis.''

''They took the teacups?''

''Good china, everyday ironstone and the flatware.''

''That does present a problem, doesn't it?'' Diana thought for a moment. ''I promised the girls I'd call for a pizza for dinner. Why don't you join us?''

''Oh, dear, I simply could not.''

Diana took in the woman's trembling hands and ashen color. ''Frankly, Mrs. Geller, I don't think you're in any condition to drive at the moment.''

''I'm fine,'' the woman said, starting toward the foyer and the front door. ''I really must be on my way, before anything else happens.''

''What more could possibly happen?'' asked Diana with a laugh. ''The only things left to repossess are the toilet seats and Cleopatra's barge-bed upstairs.''

Mrs. Geller murmured something under her breath that sounded like an old and desperate prayer. ''Mr. McClellan should be horsewhipped!'' she exclaimed, stabbing at the air with an index finger. ''Gambling and drinking away his money, then expecting good people such as you to pay the price. Dreadful, dreadful man.''

"Things happen, Mrs. Geller. Even without furniture, Gull Cottage is magnificent."

"God bless you, Ms. Travis, and good luck. This should be quite a month for you."

Diana thought of the twins, the cat, the bird, the paper shark, the empty rooms and the thirty days that stretched out before her and grinned. "Don't worry, Mrs. Geller. I have everything under control."

THE GIRLS' STOMACHS were filled with pizza and their heads with bedtime stories two hours later, when Diana tucked them into their makeshift beds on the solarium floor. A soft, summer breeze wafted in through the open French doors, and the sound of the surf crashing against the shore below was more soothing than a lullaby. As marvelous as that barge of a bed upstairs was, there was no way on earth Diana would ever get a wink's sleep, worrying that Kath or Jenny might possibly roll off the mattress and down to the floor a few thousand feet below. In fact, she wished there were crib bars along the sides, because she wasn't entirely sure she trusted herself to stay put. There was something definitely daunting about sleeping a mile or two above the place where you left your bedroom slippers.

Mr. McClellan obviously liked to live dangerously, and she couldn't help but wonder what manner of dangerous living that marvelous old bed had seen. A quick and erotic vision of her tall-dark-and-handsome knight in the black Corvette appeared, and she stubbornly willed it away. No point in wishing for the impossible, was there?

Getting the girls down for the night had been as exhausting as a four-mile run in the park, but Diana had enjoyed every minute. Seeing them shiny and pink after their bath, breathing in that baby powder smell, dressing them in their bright red sleepers—well, it was even better than seeing your byline in every major paper in the country.

"Dee Dee?" Kath's voice, sleepy and soft, drifted over to where Diana stood by the open door.

"What, honey?"

"...love you...."

Her heart did a funny kind of double thump inside her chest. "I love you, too, sweetie. Now go to sleep."

Did Paula have any idea how lucky she was? A husband, a home, two beautiful, healthy little girls whose idea of good fortune was a warm meal and a hug—all the things Diana had finally realized were there for the asking, if she'd only make up her mind she wanted them.

Well, her mind was made up. She was secure in her career, secure in who and what she was, and absolutely positive that marriage and motherhood were the next frontier and she herself the perfect pioneer.

Quietly she slipped onto the deck and stretched out in the lounge chair that the repo men had somehow forgotten to take to the great auction in the sky. The house was large and, thank God, the utilities were still operating; McClellan had had the decency to make certain his tenants had water and power, if not furniture. Diana's stack of work notes and her portable computer rested in a box in the corner of what once had been the family room, and it wouldn't take a great deal of effort to set everything up and make a list of what needed to be accomplished tomorrow.

But then she glanced out toward the beach below, where moonlight danced across the waves and the sand shimmered silver in the glow.

"Tomorrow," she said with a sigh. "I'll start tomorrow."

THE MAN was tall, dark and handsome, and Diana was nothing if not willing. His eyes glittered like sapphires, as he swept her into his arms and carried her up the walkway into the two-story Colonial house with the picket fence and the roses and the—

"Call 911! I'm having a heart attack!"

Wait a minute! What kind of fantasy dream was this, anyway?

Diana closed her eyes tighter and struggled to conjure up

Mr. Wonderful from the little store on the north fork once again. Okay, there he was and there *she* was, all safe and secure in his brawny arms as she smiled benevolently down upon the 2.5 children, who—

"Ack! My chest! My arm! Cardiac infarction! 911 fast, or I'm a dead man!"

Diana sat straight up in the lounge chair, her own heart pounding wildly inside her chest. Someone was in the house and—dear God in heaven!—the girls were alone in there with him.

Stay calm...she had to stay calm. What on earth had she put into last month's column on fifty nifty ways to foil a burglar? Forty-nine of them said in no uncertain terms: "Don't go into the house."

Unfortunately Mother, in her infinite wisdom, hadn't come equipped with two toddlers to protect.

Diana leaped to her feet and searched quickly for something she could use as a weapon. A huge, wooden pepper mill rested atop a gas grille at the far end of the deck. Grabbing it, she slipped into the solarium. The twins—thank you, God, I'll never miss another Sunday—slept blissfully on their makeshift bedding. Ignatius, to her surprise, was curled up near the copper-hooded fireplace. Boris, however, was wide-awake and watching her.

She held her finger to her lips and was about to whisper "Shh!" when she realized she was attempting to reason with a bird whose IQ was probably that of a one-year-old child. *Be quiet, Boris,* she warned silently, *or you're in line for Thanksgiving dinner.*

From somewhere in the vastness of Gull Cottage came the tinkling of wind chimes. Had the prowler climbed through a window on the second floor and suffered a coronary in the process? Okay, maybe she wasn't in the best of shape right now herself, but at least she wasn't calling for the paramedics.

But then neither was anyone else, she thought as she crept toward the center staircase, her hand clutching the pepper mill. Had he died? Was he sprawled on the floor in the master bedroom, gasping for air? Did she even remember one quarter of all she'd learned when she took the CPR and YOU course at the Stony Brook campus of New York's state university last year?

A stair board creaked beneath her bare feet, and she cringed, half expecting a quartet of prowlers to come barreling down the steps to cart her off into white slavery. What on earth were the ethics involved in saving the life of a felon, anyway?

"Such pain! What a world...what a world...."

What on earth were the odds she was losing her mind? It sounded as though the Wicked Witch from *The Wizard of Oz* was having a heart attack in the solarium.

The solarium?

Quickly Diana made her way back into the room.

"911!" Boris ordered, the second she came through the doorway. "Cardiac infarction!"

She didn't know whether to laugh or cry.

"Keep it down, Boris!" she cautioned, praying the girls wouldn't wake up. "This isn't a rerun of *Saint Elsewhere*, you know."

"My chest!" screeched the mynah bird. "The pain is excruciating!"

Excruciating? The bird had a better vocabulary than most people Diana knew. Life around Gull Cottage must be rather interesting when Laurence McClellan was in residence, if it gave mynah birds the speech patterns of a hypochondriacal Lord Olivier.

"Never last the night," Boris warned, his voice thready and sepulchral.

"Go to sleep," Diana soothed, wondering what the avian equivalent of a warm glass of milk was. "You're fine."

Boris continued to grumble, adding "...headache... backache...angina..." to his catalog of complaints. Diana ran upstairs and rummaged around in the huge linen closet for something to drape over the bird cage. It seemed criminal to toss a Porthault sheet over a buzzard, but there were times when beggars could not be choosers.

Boris, however, had other ideas, and continued his litany of ailments until the sun rose over the Atlantic, and Diana's resistance to that litany finally lowered.

"My knees hurt," groaned Boris.

"You don't *have* knees," said Diana, stifling a yawn. "They can't possibly hurt."

In answer, Boris sneezed twice and followed up with a rib-busting cough.

"I'm not impressed," said Diana, wishing his repertoire included sleep. "You're nothing but a feathery hypochondriac."

Boris let loose with an ear-splitting scream, worthy of a Grade Z horror movie, and the twins stirred beneath their Snoopy blankets.

Jenny, the animal lover of the two, sat up, her blue eyes wide. "Birdie sick?"

"I don't know, honey. He—"

"The pain! Have you no pity?" screeched Boris, flapping his wings and hopping from perch to perch. "911! 911!"

Kath sat up and rubbed her eyes. "Birdie sick?"

"Birdie sick," intoned Boris, his voice mournful.

The twins looked at Diana as if she were Vlad the Impaler. "Doctor," said Jenny, nodding wisely. "Birdie sick."

Diana looked over at Boris. "I'd love to introduce you to Frank Perdue," she mumbled under her breath, then turned to the girls. How do you explain the concept of hypochondria to a pair of two-year-old girls? "I don't think Boris is really sick. He just likes to pretend he is."

Boris, with his inimitable timing, chose that moment to emit a bloodcurdling groan, and the girls burst into sympathetic tears.

"Call the doctor!" shrieked the mynah over the wailing of the twins.

"Call the doctor!" parroted the girls.

"I know you're a fraud, Boris," Diana said, glaring at the

feathery menace, "and I know you're trying to make a fool out of me."

And doing a pretty darned good job of it, actually. The truth was, she had no choice but to call the veterinarian named in the voluminous packet of instructions attached to Boris's cage. What kind of example in human compassion would she be giving her nieces if she ignored the bird's plaintive cries for medical attention, no matter how bogus they might be?

"Call the doctor!" ordered Boris.

"Call the doctor!" ordered the girls.

"Call the doctor," said Diana. Ignatius purred his way into the room, and Diana motioned toward the feathered dictator. "Hors d'oeuvres, anyone?"

IF DAVE hadn't been so tired from yet another false alarm, Gregory would have sent his partner out to Gull Cottage to check on Boris, but the sight of the young man, yawning and gulping black coffee as he drooped over the credenza, gave Gregory pause.

"I can take it for you," said Dave through another monster yawn. "I figured it was time for Boris to put his latest caretaker through her paces. Neurotic hunk of feathers...."

"I like Boris," Gregory said blandly, thinking about Diana Travis and the look of surprise that would be on her lovely face when he showed up at the door.

"If I weren't so tired, I'd come with you. There has to be more going on at Gull Cottage than Boris's antics. I've never seen you eager to make a house call before."

"Just keeping my hand in," said Gregory, grabbing his car keys from atop the reception desk. "Mary Ann will be in at eight. Just hang on until then."

"Easier said than done," Dave mumbled. "Easier said than done...."

Gregory was still laughing as he crossed the dew-laden front lawn to the parking lot. He'd seen a lot of beautiful places, back in his quasi-celebrity days, but few of those came close to the tranquil beauty of early morning on the east end of Long Island. The air was still cool, and the sharp, salt tang of the Atlantic worked like a boost of adrenaline. His body sprang to life, and he wished he had the time for a run along the beach, working his muscles to blissful exhaustion.

The sound of Diana Travis's low, musical voice curled itself inside his ear, and other forms of blissful exhaustion offered themselves up for his inspection.

"Married, with kids," he mumbled, climbing into the 'Vette and gunning the engine.

Definitely off limits when it came to summertime romance.

He thought of her round, full breasts, and the shadowy cleavage not even her demure, Victorian dress could conceal. He thought of her small waist and how it led intriguingly into rounded hips and hidden pleasures.

He thought of a husband with a pit bull and a loaded rifle.

Sorry, Boris. Next time I'm sending Dave.

DIANA LEANED FORWARD and eyed Boris. "You're a fraud, aren't you? You're trying to make a monkey out of me."

Boris stared back at her, silent as a stone.

"Come on, Boris, don't be shy. What is it now: heart attack? Phlebitis? Don't you want me to call 911?"

Nothing. That pile of black feathers looked at Diana as if she were a cage cover.

Iggy, who was perched on a ledge near the fireplace, watched the proceedings with the smug expression of all natural aristocrats.

The front doorbell chimed with tones worthy of Westminster Abbey. "Just a cough, Boris," she pleaded, racing for the door. "A sneeze, a little angina—something!"

Anything to keep her from looking the fool in front of some snooty East End vet, who probably catered only to pedigrees whose ancestors came over on the Mayflower. The bell chimed again. Impatient, wasn't he? Quickly she smoothed down her hair, gave a tug to her tank top and opened the door.

"I'm sorry, I—" She stopped and stared up at her movie-star-handsome guide from the night before. "What on earth are *you* doing here?"

"Not a morning person, I take it, Ms. Travis?" He took in her shorts and bare legs and tank top in a glance, and she resisted the urge to hide behind the massive front door.

"Look, I don't think this is very funny. If you don't get back in that car of yours by the time I count to three, I'll call the police." *I don't care how gorgeous you are. Weird is weird.* She tilted her head to one side and glared up at him. "Did you say 'Ms. Travis'?"

"Afraid so."

"Don't tell me you're—"

"Gregory Stewart."

"The vet?"

"Boris's best friend."

"I thought you ran that store on the north shore."

"Volunteer work. One day a week."

"You're really the vet?"

"Want to feel my stethoscope?"

Dangerous question. Laughter bubbled up in her throat. "You have a way with words, I'll grant you that."

He reached into the black bag he was carrying, pulled out a regulation-issue stethoscope and placed it in her hand. "Now do you believe me?"

Before she could answer, the twins toddled over to the doorway.

"Birdie sick," said Jenny, tugging at his pants leg. Kath clutched a small box of cornflakes and nodded in agreement.

"They believe me," said Gregory Stewart.

"They're two years old."

"Where's Boris? In the solarium, as usual?"

She hesitated. "How do you—?"

"Did he say he was having a cardiac infarction?"

"Yes, but—"

"Call 911 or he's a dead man?"

"Yes." Diana hesitated. "I don't know what to believe, but I know most men don't travel around with stethoscopes and dog biscuits." She flung the door open wide. "I give up. Come on in."

"I can't move," he said as she headed toward the solarium. "They won't let go."

She turned and saw her nieces unabashedly clutching his kneecaps and beaming up at him in girlish admiration. "Kath! Jenny! Leave the nice man alone."

They upped the wattage on their baby-toothed smiles, and Diana swooped them—and the cereal box—up into her arms, grunting at their combined weight.

"I think they like me," Gregory Stewart said, tugging at one of Jenny's golden curls.

"They like *all* men," Diana said, heading once again toward the solarium. "They're incorrigible flirts." They also had splendid taste; Dr. Stewart was easily the most glorious male it had ever been Diana's pleasure to behold. Where some men's sex appeal was restrained, hidden behind a three-piece suit, Gregory's was unabashed. His blue-green eyes flashed with it; his perfect, white teeth gleamed with it; his muscular body rippled with it. He was MAN in capital letters, and Diana would be the first to say, *"Vive la différence!"*

She stopped at the entry to the solarium and inclined her head toward King Boris in his chrome-and-brass castle. "Your patient awaits," she said, then turned to leave.

"You're not staying?"

"Far be it from me to come between a man and his stethoscope."

"What if I need help restraining Boris?"

She grinned at him over her shoulder. "Call 911. I'm sure Boris won't mind."

His rumbling, baritone laugh followed her all the way to the kitchen. "Not bad, girls," she murmured as she sat them down on the shiny, tiled floor. "Not bad at all."

If only it were Labor Day and she were ten pounds lighter,

two shades blonder and officially ready to embark on her great husband hunt. Dr. Stewart would have more than the twins to worry about....

OF COURSE, there was absolutely nothing wrong with Boris the Bad—at least nothing that a little attention wouldn't cure. After listening to the bird's heartbeat and asking him to open his beak and say "Ah," Gregory checked the condition of the cage, the food, the water—and pronounced the mynah hale and hearty and destined to live to be a hundred.

"You miss Laurence, don't you?" he asked, chucking the bird under the chin and laughing as he dodged a jab from a pointed beak. "That's what all this is about, isn't it?"

"Mine not to question why," said Boris, hopping to the far end of his cage. "Mine but to do or die."

"Not while I'm your doctor, pal." Gregory put his stethoscope back in his bag and snapped it shut.

"Thank you," said Boris as Gregory turned to leave. "Y'all come back now, hear?"

No one was in the huge foyer, the living room or the dining room, but Gregory caught the sounds of laughter from somewhere in the rear of the house, so he followed the trail of cornflakes to the sun-filled kitchen, where he found Diana Travis.

The two little girls sat near the back door eating cereal. Diana was bent low over them, her blond curls glittering in the morning sunlight. Her skin was smooth and tinted a pale apricot—cheeks, arms, the long, lithe expanse of leg bared by her shorts, all of it the same delicate shade. It wasn't hard to imagine that she was the same glorious apricot all over, juicy and ripe and—   *Married.*

Keep that in mind, Stewart. This woman looks as married as you can get.

Those two little girls of hers weren't the product of Central Casting, and he'd be doing himself a favor if he kept reminding himself of that fact.

She leaned over to retrieve a plastic spoon, and her top

rode up, revealing the inward curve of her waist. He wished he was standing near the back door, because he had the feeling the view from that angle would be even more intriguing. She had the kind of body that women's magazines hated—and men dreamed about. Ripe. Touchable. An exciting combination of curves and possibilities that was—

Married.

Right.

"Ms. Travis?" He stepped into the room, feeling large and male and decidedly out of place.

Diana turned quickly and looked at him, her hazel eyes wide with anxiety. "How bad is it?"

"Not bad at all. Poor old guy's beak is out of joint."

"He's looking for attention?"

"Exactly. With Laurence roaming around the world and strangers coming in and out, Boris is voicing his displeasure."

"Rather forcefully, I'd say."

"Mynahs aren't known for shyness."

"Where on earth did he learn terms like cardiac infarction?"

"Have you ever met Laurence?"

She shook her head.

"Laurence McClellan is a first-class worrier. Rumor has it he's claimed everything from dysentery to beriberi to a four-alarm heart attack."

"Is there anything wrong with him?"

"Not a thing. He and Boris are both hale and healthy and hypochondriacal."

"So I don't have to administer CPR to Boris?"

"Just feed him and talk to him. That's all it takes."

"If there's one thing I'm good at, it's administering TLC." She gestured toward the corpulent cat stretching in the sunshine near the door. "See what I mean?"

"Afraid so. What would you say to a medically supervised feline diet?"

"I'd say it's between you and Ignatius. I have my own avoirdupois to contend with."

There was an awkward silence, punctuated only by the sound of the two little girls crunching dry cereal and sprinkling the crumbs on top of the cat. He wanted to say she looked pretty damn good to him, but knew it would sound like the worst kind of come-on since "hubba-hubba." Besides, there was his hard and fast rule about married women.

Diana shifted from one foot to the other, then broke the silence. "Thanks for coming by so early. Even TV repairmen don't make house calls these days. Your kind is a dying breed."

He offered a mock salute. "It's part of the job, ma'am."

"How much do I owe you?"

"Nothing. Larry keeps me on retainer. His office will pay me."

"Lots of luck, Dr. Stewart," she said. "Mr. McClellan doesn't seem to be in the greatest shape financially."

He glanced around the empty room. "There's no furniture in here."

"You just noticed? There's also no furniture in the solarium, the living room, the dining room, and all points east, west and north."

"You rented an empty mansion?"

"Not exactly. This was a surprise development."

"You're a good sport."

"You're the second person to say that. I'm beginning to wonder if I should be more upset."

"What does your husband have to say about it?"

"Not much, I would imagine. He's too busy, getting ready to marry his prepubescent bride."

Despite himself, Gregory's eyes widened. "Did I miss something?"

"We're divorced," she said, taking the cereal box away from the little girls. "He's giving up his hard-won freedom on Independence Day."

"He has a sense of humor."

"Not so I ever noticed."

"Your daughters look just like you."

That impish grin of hers reappeared. "Their mother won't appreciate that. My sister thinks they're her clones."

"I'm getting extremely confused." Not to mention hopeful.

"I'm baby-sitting," she said, pouring cereal into one of the Fraggle Rock cups on the countertop. "Paula and Art ended up in Monte Carlo instead of the Hamptons. I inherited their vacation and their daughters for the month."

He whistled low. "Gull Cottage for a month. Not too shabby, even without furniture."

"I don't want to keep you from your breakfast, Doctor. Your wife must be waiting for you."

"No wife."

"Divorced?"

"Never married." She looked surprised and he laughed. "Heterosexual," he said. "Irredeemably, I might add."

"How wonderful for you," she murmured, pouring cereal into a Sesame Street soup bowl.

"Now and then, it has been." He'd spent a lot of energy a few years ago proving to himself that he was as hale, hearty, and healthy as everyone else believed.

She met his eyes and couldn't hold back her answering smile. "No girlfriend waiting up for you with fresh coffee and croissants?"

"No girlfriend."

"I don't suppose you'd like to stay for breakfast."

"Am I invited?"

"Yes, but—"

"Thanks," he said, reaching for a Fraggle Rock cup and a plastic spoon. "Don't mind if I do."

Chapter Six

"You're kidding." The words were out before Diana could stop them. "You really will stay for breakfast?"

His eyes narrowed. "You're rescinding the offer?"

"No, nothing like that. I just didn't expect you to say yes." She gestured toward the bowl of cornflakes on the countertop. "This isn't exactly gourmet fare I'm offering you."

"I'm easy to please."

"Why is it I doubt that? You strike me as the eggs Benedict type."

"Where'd you get that idea?"

"The Corvette. The expensive watch. The Ralph Lauren shirt." *The fact that you have* privileged *written all over your gorgeous face....*

"Don't hold the shirt against me. It was a birthday present, from a friend who thought I should dress more East End."

She glanced down at her own cutoffs and faded tank top. "Like me?" she asked with a rueful grin.

His gaze traveled slowly up her body, warming her calves and knees, lingering on her thighs, then gliding over hips and breasts until he met her eyes. It was a wonder she didn't spontaneously combust.

"Like you," he said, his voice lazy and sexually charged. "You look good to me."

The man was amazing. For a moment she felt positively

beautiful. "I doubt if the Ralph Lauren set would agree with you."

"Public opinion means that much to you?"

She poured cereal into his cup and her own, then took the milk out of the almost bare refrigerator. "Actually, I live for public opinion."

"What are you, a politician?"

"No." She took a deep breath. "I'm Mother."

"I thought these kids were your sister's."

"They are. I mean, I'm Mother Knows Best."

"I thought Mother was a seventy-year-old lady with gray hair and sensible shoes."

"Thanks a lot. We were aiming for warm and maternal."

He took another assessing look at her. "You don't exactly look like the happy homemaker type."

"Everyone thinks I look like someone's wife or sister or mother. It was inevitable that I turned it into a profession."

"You didn't exactly have a handle on things yesterday when you came looking for a bathroom."

She thought about her stained Laura Ashley dress, the baby wipes she'd sent him out for, and the missing red sneaker. "That wasn't me yesterday. I'm basically an organized, competent person."

He arched a brow.

"I'll have you know I'm a magician with a Handi-Wipe."

"I'm having trouble believing this," he said, spooning up some cereal. "I saw you on TV a few years ago. You had gray hair and glasses."

"That was my mother. Mother was the first Mother Knows Best. She specialized in writing columns about my father's military approach to housekeeping."

"Didn't she go on Johnny Carson once and recommend keeping an egg timer on the bathroom sink?"

"We won't go into that," said Diana, remembering the toothbrushing speed drills the General had been so fond of. "My parents both believed in a place for everything and everything in its place—as fast as humanly possible."

Quickly she explained how her mother had handed over "Mother Knows Best" to her struggling daughter to fulfill the last months of the syndication contract, only to have Diana turn it into a full-blown phenomenon practically overnight.

The gorgeous Dr. Stewart swallowed his cereal. "You give sexual advice, don't you?" He reached out and stilled her hand, drawing her eyes to his.

Her cheeks warmed. "Only in the nicest way."

"Last week you recommended lighting candles in the bedroom."

"Strictly to cut down on power costs." *And the better to see you with, Dr. Wonderful....*

"What about the perfume on the light bulbs?"

"More efficient than room freshener." *L'Air du Temps, strategically placed on each of her pounding pulse points for him to discover one by one by one....*

"You're a practical woman."

"I believe in prioritizing."

"I hate words like 'prioritize.'"

"You're extraordinarily opinionated for a man who makes house calls on mynah birds."

"Are you always this touchy? Talking to you is like sitting on a cactus."

She considered him for a moment, then threw caution to the winds. "You weren't exactly the most hospitable of hosts last evening."

"I brought you the baby wipes, didn't I?"

"You seemed annoyed."

"I was annoyed. You had me blocked in the driveway."

"I moved, didn't I?"

"Took you long enough. I thought I'd have to call for a tow truck to get you out of there." He grinned broadly. "Where's the egg timer when you really need it?"

"In my overnight bag. Mother aims to please."

"I know. I read your column on fifty ways to lure a lover."

"Now I know why so many writers hide behind pseudonyms. Maybe I should have tackled a gardening column."

"And waste your natural resources?"

"If that's a polite way of telling me I'm fat—"

"Fat?" He looked genuinely puzzled. "You look great."

"Great is a size six."

"You're not one of those bean-sprouts and strained-yogurt types, are you?"

"I wouldn't be size ten if I were, Doctor."

"Gregory."

Was she crazy, or did she hear the faint, but highly exciting sound of a Scottish burr? A smile twitched at the corners of her mouth. "Diana."

"Boris has a habit of bringing people together."

"I promise to keep it to a minimum."

"McClellan wouldn't like it if Boris's needs were neglected."

"I'll be a slave to his every whim." She glanced down at her hand, still held firmly in his. Delightful it was, but growing awkward. "As a matter of fact, I should begin by learning where the local birdseed store is located."

He noted her glance and released her hand. "No problem."

She reached for the notebook propped up near the stove. "I also need a supermarket, a video store, a bank and a post office?"

He snapped his fingers. "Nothing to it. I'll show you."

Her heart fluttered foolishly, as if this were something more than a mild flirtation as practiced by a man who was obviously an expert in the art. This proved just how out of touch with life she'd become, buried under Mother's ample skirts, writing about freezer burn and ring around the collar.

"I come as a package deal," she said, gesturing toward the girls, who were covered in cornflakes and milk.

"I realize that."

"I only have two hours to shop."

"I'll take what I can get." He put a sexual twist on his

words that had her wondering whether to call the vice squad or just save time and surrender. She watched as he quickly drew a map and handed it to her. "Meet me at the animal hospital in an hour and a half."

"You don't have to do this, Gregory," she demurred.

He took a step toward her. "I made myself a promise a few years ago not to do anything I don't want to do. I haven't broken it yet." There was a flash of menace hidden in that movie-star-gorgeous face. "If you want my help, say so."

Say no, her common sense warned. *Get out while you still can.* She was there for work, not romance. She wasn't ready for romance. She wouldn't *be* ready for romance until Labor Day. "Ten o'clock," she said after a moment. "The animal hospital."

"Good," he said, heading toward the door.

"Crazy," she said, locking it behind him.

"No fool like an old fool," called out Boris from the solarium.

At that moment, Diana was in full agreement.

IT WAS CHAOS as usual, back at the East End Animal Hospital. Dave and Peggy's baby had once again decided to stay put and Dave, wide-awake and anxious, was running some blood work in the lab. Daisy also had yet to deliver and she thumped her tail lazily as Gregory raced into the office after leaving Gull Cottage.

"You look lousy," said Mary Ann Marino as he bent down to stroke Daisy behind the ear. "Bad night at Black Rock?"

"Emergency call from our friend Boris." He nodded his thanks as she handed him a cup of steaming, black coffee.

"What was it this time: heart attack or an aching back?"

"Cardiac infarction."

Mary Ann rubbed her hands together in mock glee. "The old boy's getting inventive. I like that."

"Damn bird has a better medical vocabulary than I have."

"I'm surprised McClellan fell for Boris's malarkey again."

"McClellan's out of town, remember? Gull Cottage is being rented."

"Oh, yeah. Ms. Piper, isn't it, and all those wonderful show-business types?"

"The show-business types are gone."

Mary Ann arched a brow. "Boris made the call himself?"

"You are one nosy woman, Marino."

She sat atop her desk, looking for all the world like a star-struck adolescent. "I won't make a scene—you can trust me. Who is it? Tom Cruise? Mel Gibson? Sean and Madonna?"

"A woman, two kids and a cat."

"Where's her husband?"

"Doesn't have one."

"Single mother, and she can afford a month at Club Paradise? I'd like to compare child support checks with her."

"They're not her kids. Her brother-in-law rented the place, and she's here to work."

Mary Ann narrowed her eyes and pretended to concentrate. "Don't tell me—let me guess. She's five feet, seven inches tall, blond and beautiful, and you've appointed yourself her guardian-protector."

"She's blond, she's small, and the rest is none of your business."

Her blue eyes, so like her son's in expression, twinkled and Gregory ruffled her curly, red bangs.

"I'm going to shave and change my shirt," he said. "Hold the fort."

Mary Ann muttered something unprintable, and laughing, he headed for his office in the back.

It didn't take long to change into clean clothes or to comb his unruly, black hair. He ran a hand along the underside of his jaw and felt the quill-like bristles of a day's growth of beard. Unless he wanted to look like a Don Johnson also-ran, he'd better do something about that, so he headed back into the tiny office bathroom, pulled a straight razor and shaving cream from the medicine cabinet and set to work.

She's not your type, he thought as he maneuvered the blade along the angle of his jaw.

He liked tall, willowy brunettes with eyes the color of melted caramels.

Diana Travis was small and round and a hazel-eyed blonde.

He liked women who wore slinky, black dresses and kept their emotions as banked as their trust funds.

Diana Travis wore cotton and cutoffs and seemed to live on the edge of collapse.

He swore, and grabbed a piece of tissue to press against the cut on his chin. His body screamed for sleep; his stomach rumbled for real food; his eyes were crossed with fatigue. If he had any brains at all, he'd be stretched out in his airconditioned bedroom, grabbing some needed rest, not getting ready to play tour guide to a summer renter who was everything he wasn't looking for in a woman.

But then what was he looking for in a woman, anyway? There had been so many after Hayley left, as if he'd had to prove himself over and over again in a variety of ways, searching for answers he could never find anywhere but inside his own soul. After a while the fiery need to reaffirm his own life had cooled, and although he hadn't been celibate this last year, he'd been close to it.

Hell, he wasn't looking for a woman at all. He was only looking to get out. He didn't want to leave anyone behind when he left, no broken hearts or empty promises or any of the myriad complications that came with modern romance.

The last thing he wanted was someone like Diana with those sparkling eyes, that soft voice and tempting body.

"Damn!" he swore as he nicked himself again and reached for the styptic pencil on the edge of the sink.

"Talking to yourself, are you?" asked Mary Ann from the doorway. "Not a good sign."

"Eavesdropping again, are you?" he countered, wielding

the razor in the space between his nose and his upper lip. "Not a good sign either, M.A." He rinsed the blade in the sink, then glanced at her in the mirror. "Did Joey tell you about the beer?"

"Leading my kid down the path to perdition, are you, Greg? First it's beer. Next it's a bachelor pad and the Playmate of the Month."

"He hated it, M.A. I caught him rinsing out his mouth with Pepsi." Gregory put away the razor and shaving cream, then dried his face on a whisper-thin towel.

"He didn't tell me that part."

"He wouldn't. I'm violating a major tenet of male bonding by telling you this much."

"What are we going to do when you leave, Greg? Who's going to explain all that macho business to him?"

"You'll manage. You always have." He gave her a hug, then willed himself to ignore the sudden stab of guilt her teasing words had caused. He'd waited a long time for this; he deserved it in a way Mary Ann couldn't possibly understand.

Come August 15, he was out of there.

Nothing was about to change that fact, not even Joey Marino.

Not even Diana Travis.

"I DON'T THINK your receptionist likes me," said Diana as she climbed into her rented station wagon to head back into East Hampton. It was five after ten, and she was feeling inordinately pleased with herself.

"It's nothing personal." Gregory turned and gave a final tug at each of the girls' safety harnesses, then looked back at her. "Mary Ann doesn't like anybody these days."

"She seems to like you well enough."

"It's payday and she's a practical woman. If she said something to upset you, I'd be glad to speak with her about it. Mary Ann has the habit of speaking her mind, whether you want to hear it or not."

"It's not that she said anything exactly," said Diana, starting the engine. "It's more what she didn't say."

"Maybe it's your imagination."

"I'm not a terribly imaginative woman, Gregory. That's why I write the kind of column I do."

"It takes a hell of a mind to come up with one hundred things to do with chopsticks."

"What it takes is a sense of humor. I know your receptionist doesn't like me."

"Mary Ann has a lot on her mind lately. Trust me, when I say it's nothing personal."

Diana nodded, not about to argue with him about his receptionist's private life. If he wanted to believe the woman was frowning over what to cook for dinner, that was his business. Diana, however, was a firm believer in woman's intuition, and she knew there had been a great deal more than simple curiosity in the redhead's face.

Gregory balked about fastening his seat belt, but Diana refused to back out of her parking spot until he did.

"You're worse than my mother," he groused.

"Thank you," she said. "Mother takes that as a compliment. Seat belts save lives."

"So does using the brakes," he said, wincing as she rolled to a stop at the traffic light on Route 27A West. "You might want to give it a shot."

"You don't give an inch on anything, do you?"

"Life's too short to compromise."

"I agree that life's too short, but compromise makes it run smoother, wouldn't you say?"

"Spoken by a woman who's probably never compromised on anything in her entire life."

"An unfair assumption," Diana said as she drove past the Hook Mill and into East Hampton proper. "You don't know the first thing about me."

"Name one major item you've compromised on in your life."

"Gull Cottage," she said, glancing into her rearview mirror at the twins, who were busy playing with their stuffed dinosaurs. "I'm living there without furniture. I'd say that qualifies as a major league compromise."

"Doesn't count. You said your brother-in-law paid for and okayed the deal. You're just going along with it for the ride."

"I hate men with perfect memories," she muttered. "I'm still there."

"I've been wondering about that," he said. "Why *are* you still there?"

"Beats Holiday Inn."

"They have furniture at Holiday Inn. Televisions, alarm clocks, all the modern conveniences."

"I'll have all the modern conveniences, too, once I finish shopping."

"Seems like a lot of trouble to go through for a month by the water. I would have stayed home."

"Great idea, if you have one."

He didn't even try to hide his curiosity. "You don't look like one of the homeless to me."

"I am," she said, stopping at another traffic signal, "although it's by choice, not circumstance. I've moved around a great deal the past few years. My last lease ran out a few weeks ago, and I've been staying at an inn in Bucks County."

"Wanderlust?" he asked, watching her profile closely as the light turned green.

"You could call it that. It seemed as good a cure for the post-divorce blues as any other I could come up with."

"Did it work?"

"I think so. I'll know for sure after the Fourth of July, when he marries his pregnant, pom-pom queen."

"Jealous?"

"Yes," said Diana honestly, aware of the intensity of his gaze. "I guess I am."

"Still love him?"

The answer, of course, was none of Dr. Gregory Stewart's business. "No, I don't, but I envy what they have together."

"Home? Marriage? Baby on the way?"

"All of the above," said Diana. All of the things she'd taken for granted when she was young and foolish. "It took me a while to realize it. Now I have to make up for lost time."

"What would people think if they knew Mother didn't have a home of her own?"

"I'm trusting you to keep it secret. The public doesn't need to know everything."

"Your secret's safe with me. Doctor-patient privilege."

"You're a vet."

"And you're Boris's guardian for the month. It's all in the family."

He was tall, dark and handsome; he was good with kids and he had a sense of humor. She was overweight and over-tired, taking care of two kids and working toward a deadline. There was no justice in the world. She was about to tell him exactly that, when he directed her off Main Street and she pulled into the parking lot by the A and P.

It took a little time to get Kath and Jenny set up in their double stroller, but finally they were ready to embark on the great shopping expedition.

"Where to first?" he asked. "Supermarket? Bank? Post office?"

"The video store," said Diana.

"What about food?"

"You have your priorities. I have mine. If I'm going to survive a month with the Bobbsey Twins, I'd better be able to provide *Sesame Street*, the Smurfs, and a daily dose of Walt Disney."

Gregory Stewart turned out to be better than a Mobil Travel Guide. He seemed to know every inch of East Hampton, and in short order Diana had a working familiarity with the picturesque town that reminded her of Norman Rockwell's idea of a perfect, New England village.

But there was more to East Hampton than just its pretty face—or its trendy status. Thanks to Gregory Stewart, she could imagine the vicious winters during the Revolutionary War, when British troops camped out on the village green, stole a pot of suet pudding and tossed it down the hill, now aptly named Pudding Hill. Once the village green had been home to hundreds of honking geese, and the South End Burying Ground had provided grazing pastures for wandering cows, as well as a final resting place for the town's citizens.

And, of course, there were the glorious turn-of-the-century summers when the crème de la crème of New York society discovered the bucolic pleasures of the tiny town and made it famous.

Young artists had gathered at Rowdy Hall, studying by day and carousing by night. Diana could almost hear the sound of their long-ago laughter floating up from the fields where they had set up their easels. Jack and Janet Bouvier had once rented Rowdy Hall, and little Jacqueline—one day to be Jacqueline Bouvier Kennedy Onassis—had celebrated her second birthday right there.

There were the Hook Mill, the Presbyterian churches, and "Home, Sweet Home," but unfortunately, she wasn't there to sightsee; she was there to shop, and shop she did. She rented a TV and VCR at the video store and found some old dishes at the ladies' auxiliary behind the church. In short order, she had managed to make most of her major purchases and a few minor ones, as well.

"I didn't see chocolate cheesecake on your list," Gregory said as they exited the pricey Dean and DeLuca specialty store.

Diana pushed thoughts of those extra ten pounds from her mind. "I'm a shopkeeper's dream come true," she said, struggling with her packages and the stroller.

He stopped short, his own muscular arms laden with her packages. "Give me the cheesecake."

"Can I trust you?"

"You'll have to take your chances. The rate you're going, it'll end up splattered on the sidewalk."

"Perish the thought," she said with a shiver and handed

over the precious cargo to him for safe transit. They looked as if they were ready to embark on a yearlong safari. And to think most of her purchases were being delivered to Gull Cottage later on....

Gregory piled the cheesecake atop his stack of packages, and they continued walking. There was something to be said for having a man along, she thought as they walked down the broad, tree-lined street past jewelry stores and bookshops and one adorable boutique after another.

Actually there was something to be said for having this particular man along. She'd been shameless, the way she watched him that morning, enjoying the play of sunlight in his thick, dark hair, the sparkle in his blue-green eyes. Once when he bent down to retrieve one of Jenny's toys, Diana had found herself mesmerized by the splendid swelling of muscles crisscrossing his broad back.

She'd even felt an odd kind of female satisfaction in the way other women—of all ages—found it equally impossible to look away when Gregory was in the room. Diana had never thought herself prone to foolishness like that, but apparently the opportunity simply hadn't presented itself before now.

To make matters even more amazing, he was as agreeable as he was gorgeous. He had sweet-talked the twins out of a major temper tantrum in the bank; he had orchestrated a terrific deal on a card table and chairs; he had even procured the best possible rental fee at the local video store without so much as raising his voice. Mother couldn't have done better herself.

And she'd be lying, if she said having an extra pair of strong arms around to share the burden didn't make life considerably sweeter.

The sun was hot and bright overhead, cooled by the salty breeze blowing in from the Atlantic nearby. The spicy scent of geraniums and the sweet smell of roses wafted on the air as they strolled past a garden in full bloom, and she breathed deeply, filling her head with the delightful mixture of perfumes.

"You're a lucky man," she said, peering up at him through her dark glasses. "Living in the middle of a picture postcard all year long."

"From September to June it's terrific, but you can keep it during the season."

"I take it you don't like summer people."

"They're a necessary evil," he said with a shrug of his broad shoulders, "but I sure as hell breathe a sigh of relief after Labor Day."

A perfectly matched couple straight out of the L. L. Bean Catalog loped past them, talking—in tones worthy of Harvard and Yale—about the perfect twelve-dollar eggplant they'd discovered at Madame Makarova's Russian Deli.

"See what I mean?" Gregory said with a wry twist of his mouth.

"Afraid so," replied Diana. "The dreaded summer people. And to think I'm one of them."

"At least you're not wearing madras," he said. "I hate madras."

"One thing confuses me," she said as they turned off Main Street and headed back toward the parking lot near the A and P. "You know East Hampton like the back of your hand. You volunteer on the north fork and work on the south. Where exactly do you live—in Gardiners Bay?"

"I used to live in Southold, right near the store where you met me yesterday, but I rented out the house just before Memorial Day. I've been living behind the animal hospital ever since."

It was none of her business why he was living behind the animal hospital, any more than it was his business why she lived nowhere at all, but Diana had never been one to err on the side of caution.

"Money problems?"

He didn't bat an eye. "Scheduling problems. It was either rent the house then or forever hold my mortgage."

"Good fiscal planning."

"I thought so."

"Are you buying another house around East Hampton?"

"Actually I'm leaving East Hampton in mid-August and sailing down to the Caribbean."

"The Caribbean during the hurricane season?"

"What can I say? I like to live dangerously."

"Will you be closing the hospital down?"

"The season will be practically over by then. My partner can handle it alone until Labor Day. After that, things quiet down."

"Sailing down to the Caribbean," she said, whistling low. "Lucky man."

He looked at her for a long moment before he spoke. "Yeah," he said, stretching the word out then snapping it back into place like a perfectly aimed slingshot. "That's me."

Too soon they were once again at the station wagon, loading up the back with her purchases and strapping the girls into their car seats for the ride to the animal hospital—and the end of the delightful morning.

As he fastened his own seat belt, his large hand brushed against Diana's thigh.

"Sorry," he said, meeting her gaze.

"No problem," she said, although that brief contact had only heightened the delicious fantasies she'd been indulging in all morning.

They chatted easily as she drove back; Diana found it hard to believe that twenty-four hours ago Gregory Stewart had been a stranger. He had a sharp wit and a quirky disposition and at times he was arrogant, to boot, but she enjoyed his company and finally stopped worrying about her extra pounds and the fact her hair looked as if she'd stuck her finger into a light socket.

She turned left into the circular driveway that led to the veterinary hospital and shifted the station wagon into Park.

"Here we are," she said, stating the obvious. "I don't know what I'd have done without you."

"You'd have managed, Mother," he said with an easy laugh. "It might have taken longer, but you'd have managed fine."

"You're right," she said, retrieving Kath's stuffed triceratops from the floor of the back seat, "but that doesn't mean I didn't appreciate the help."

"And the company?" Was she mad, or was there a touch of uncertainty in the gorgeous doctor's voice?

"And the company."

"If you and the twins aren't doing anything on the Fourth, I give a barbecue every year and I..." His words drifted off into a pleasant kind of mumble she found quite endearing.

"It sounds wonderful," she said cautiously, "but aren't you forgetting something? You don't have a house or a yard any longer."

"There's plenty of property behind here," he said, gesturing toward the back of the hospital building. "If the barbecue's good enough, no one will miss the ambience."

"Have it at Gull Cottage, why don't you?"

He looked as surprised as she was by her words.

"Gull Cottage," she repeated, warming to the spur-of-the-moment idea. "The place is huge. We have a barbecue grill, a swimming pool, a beach."

"It's also fancy as hell. What if something breaks?"

"The place is empty as an abandoned railroad station. The only things left of Mr. McClellan's are Boris, the papier-mâché shark, the slot machine and Cleopatra's barge. If they can survive Kath and Jenny, they can survive anything."

"Cleopatra's barge?"

"You'd have to see it to believe it." She offered him her best smile by means of encouragement. "Come on, Gregory. What do you say? You'd be doing me a real favor. I'd even supply the food."

"Supplying the mansion should be enough of a contribution."

"No, I'm serious. I have a whole chapter's worth of picnic recipes I need to test for the book I'm putting together. You and your friends could be my guinea pigs."

"Maybe we should call for the Colonel."

Her dignity was on the line, and she leaned toward him in righteous indignation. "The hapless wench you've seen the past two days isn't the real me. The least you can do is give me a chance to redeem my reputation as an organized, upstanding woman."

"I'll supply the beer and soda and ice cream."

"And the guests."

"And the guests." It wouldn't be a large gathering: his receptionist and her son; his partner and his very pregnant wife; Gregory, Diana and the girls. "You sure?"

"Positive," she said with conviction. "It's about time Mother got some hands-on experience."

"You're something else, Diana Travis. Most women would run."

"It beats sitting around, thinking of my ex-husband walking down the aisle."

"Yes," he said slowly. "I guess it does."

"Besides, the Fourth of July isn't the Fourth of July without a barbecue."

She was still leaning toward him, close enough to catch the smell of sunshine and spice that seemed to be his own unique scent. His expression changed, angled sharply down into something dark and thrilling, and for one long, shimmering moment she had the notion he might kiss her, but a car pulled into the lot next to them and the mood was broken.

"Around noon?" he asked as he climbed out of the station wagon.

"Around noon," she said, smiling broadly and shifting into drive. "Prepare to feast, Dr. Stewart. This is going to be a Fourth of July you'll never forget."

Chapter Seven

"You've lost your mind," said Paula through the crackly long-distance connection from Monte Carlo later that afternoon. "Absolutely stark raving mad."

"Speak up," said Diana, perversely. "I can barely hear you."

"I said you're nuts!" Paula yelled from her villa on the Riviera. "Inviting total strangers over for a barbecue. Whatever possessed you to do such a thing?"

"Research."

"Research? It must be the connection. You're just not making any sense, Diana."

"It would cost you two dollars a minute to have me explain, Paulie. Why don't you just take my word for it? I know what I'm doing." She'd spent the past seven minutes explaining her plans for the Fourth of July in excruciating detail to her sister, and she had no intention of doing a repeat performance.

"You don't even know the man."

"I know him well enough, and besides, McClellan must trust him: he's Boris's vet."

"How reassuring," Paula drawled. "He has a way with mynah birds."

"I think you're forgetting something very important, Paulie. I'm the sensible one. You're the flake."

"Thanks a lot."

"You're the one who rented a mansion without furniture. If I hadn't bought some things, the girls would be sleeping on the floor."

"The floor!"

"That disaster has been averted, thanks to Dr. Stewart. I have two, gorgeous, junior beds set up in the master bedroom. The girls are just fine, and will continue to be just fine until you swoop down and whisk them back home to your love nest in New Jersey. Until then, quit worrying, okay?"

Fortunately Paula's critical analysis of Diana's plans for the Fourth of July was cut short by the arrival of a phalanx of delivery men, bearing the rest of the bounty necessary for Diana's month at Gull Cottage.

By five o'clock she had cups and dishes, glasses and pots and pans, a television set and VCR, a transistor radio and a card table covered with a flannel-backed, red vinyl tablecloth. Earlier she'd discovered daisies growing rampant in a patch on the eastern side of the house, and she had picked a bunch and stuck them haphazardly into an empty soda bottle. Now that makeshift bouquet graced the center of the fold-up card table. "Little touches mean a lot," she'd written blithely, never understanding the meaning of the words. "Just a few blossoms can make a wonderful difference in your surroundings!" Once again Mother had been dead-on. She doubted that Gull Cottage had ever known such affordable elegance....

Laughter floated toward her from the solarium: Kath and Jenny's high-pitched trills, Mr. Rogers's gentle chuckle, and Boris's ear-splitting guffaw. Ignatius slept in a pool of sunshine near the card table, while dinner bubbled on the stove. Thick stacks of computer printout paper marched along the far counter, bearing every recipe she'd ever included in one of Mother's columns.

Her portable computer also sat there, but Diana averted her eyes. Cooking for the barbecue would constitute working toward her deadline, she rationalized, cadging a taste of chili from the pot. Didn't Mother owe it to her readers to taste-test her recipes, so the ''best of the best'' lived up to their name? And, Diana admitted, didn't she owe it to Gregory Stewart and his friends to give them a Fourth of July feast to remember?

There'd be plenty of time after the barbecue to get down to *real* work on her book. She'd have weeks with nothing to do but play with the girls on the beach by day and work diligently at the computer by night. Surely her schedule would survive a minor amendment. As it was, she had less than forty-eight hours to get ready for her introduction into East Hampton society.

With apologies to her editor, she sat down to make up her grocery list for the party.

JOEY'S FRECKLED FACE curled up on itself as he squeezed his eyes shut. ''Ouch!'' he said, his voice high and scared. ''That's gotta hurt.''

''It does,'' said Gregory, ''but sometimes pain is a part of life.''

''She must hate it.''

''I don't think she thinks about it one way or the other, Joey. Daisy's just doing what she's meant to do.''

Joey gave a snorting laugh and opened one brown eye to look at Gregory. ''My mom would punch you for that. She says women are more than baby machines. She says—''

''I know exactly what your mom says, and she's right, but in case you haven't noticed, Daisy's not a woman. She's a cocker spaniel.''

''She's still a girl.''

''A female, Joey. There's a distinction.''

''I don't get it.''

''You will,'' Gregory said with a chuckle. ''Soon enough.''

Why Daisy had chosen the morning of the Fourth to be delivery day was beyond Gregory, and he was glad the boy hadn't asked that question. Females were mysterious, and never more so than when embarking upon the wild seas of motherhood. The female of the species—*any* species—lived by her own rules, and the male—no matter how well schooled in biology—would never be privy to her secrets.

And so it was that Daisy's six puppies arrived two days ahead of schedule, while Dave's wife Peggy was two weeks behind. Go figure.

"Should we warm some milk or something?" Joey asked, wide-eyed, as Daisy licked the last arrival clean.

"I think Daisy can take care of the milk herself," Gregory said, rocking back on his heels as he watched the pups root around, searching for their mother's teats. "Take a look, kid. It isn't every day you get to see a miracle."

They watched quietly for a long while, the man and the boy, as Daisy adjusted to the demands of motherhood, and it wasn't until they heard the sound of Mary Ann's horn in the driveway that either remembered it was a little after dawn and they were both exhausted.

"Your mother's waiting," said Gregory as he stood up, then gave Joey a hand. "Why don't you motor, and I'll finish up around here before Charlie gets in?" Charlie was a resident in veterinary surgery who would be signing on full-time later that summer.

"Aw, she just wants me to go home and take a nap," Joey said, with a wave of his hand. "I don't need one."

"Humor her," said Gregory, tugging at the ubiquitous Yankee cap on the boy's head. "Mothers need that sometimes."

"Yeah?"

"Yeah. It's too early to show up at Gull Cottage, anyway." He forced a yawn and stretched broadly. "As a matter of fact, I wouldn't mind catching a few Zs while I wait for coverage."

Joey did his best to stifle his own yawn, but failed miserably. "Well, maybe."

"Do me a favor, pal, and go home with your mom. I'm getting too damn old for these night-shift maternity cases. If I don't get some sleep, I'll nod off during the barbecue."

"You old guys have problems like that, huh?" asked Joey, with a big grin.

"Us old guys can still run rings around you youngsters," said Gregory, walking Joey out to the front door. "Don't you forget that."

Mary Ann, dressed in pajamas and a flowered, cotton robe, sat behind the wheel of her Hyundai, puffing on a cigarette and tapping a finger on the door frame. They saw her gesture impatiently for her son to get a move on.

"You'd better hustle your butt," said Gregory. "I think she means business."

"I think she's in a bad mood," said Joey, playfully ducking behind Gregory's broad back. "You really gonna make me go home with her?"

"Better you than me, pal." He grabbed Joey by his bony shoulders and gave him a push down the driveway. "See you back here about eleven-thirty."

He waited until Mary Ann, who was never at her best that early in the morning, disappeared down the main drag, then went back inside the hospital.

Life renewing itself, Gregory thought as he turned the key in the top lock, then made his way back to the spaniel and her litter. Six times over Daisy had replaced herself on the earth, and there was something immensely moving about that fact.

Such a simple feat.

Such an incredible miracle—even for a cocker spaniel.

Such an unlikely dream.

"Damn," swore Gregory softly as he looked down at the new mother nursing her young. "Damn...."

"...AND THEN you can play in the sand." Diana ran the comb through Kath's curls one last time, while Jenny stood by watching. "How does that sound?"

"Big Bird, too?" asked Kath, who had dubbed Boris with that nickname.

Diana laughed and straightened the straps of the toddler's

red, white and blue sunsuit. "Boris can't go down to the beach, honey. He has to stay inside his cage."

"Bring cage," said Jenny, ever the practical one.

"Birds don't go to the beach," Diana repeated, leading the girls down the back stairs to the kitchen.

"Why?" asked Kath. "Seagirls do."

"Seagulls, honey." Just yesterday Diana had delivered a beachfront lecture on sea gulls and their place in the ecological scheme of things. "Sea gulls like the beach. Mynah birds don't."

"Why?" asked Jenny.

"They get sunburned," said Diana. It seemed as good a reason as any.

"Why?" asked Kath.

"I don't know," Diana admitted. "Maybe their beaks get burned. Why don't you ask Boris about it?" *Please* ask Boris about it. It would serve that arrogant batch of feathers right.

The girls giggled as they ran through the kitchen to go question Boris. Diana exhaled on a sigh. How did Paula do it day after day? she wondered. Her own daydreams of a sweet and adorable Gerber baby were a pale imitation of reality. The twins' minds seemed to race all across the board like amusement park bumper cars; when they weren't saying "No!" at the top of their lungs, they were asking "Why?"

Why was Iggy so fat? Why did he sleep so much? Why could Boris talk, while Iggy only meowed?

And why was it Diana fell asleep last night at dinner with her eyes wide open, when they were all ready to watch *Cinderella* and *Mary Poppins* in their own, private, Gull Cottage Disney Film Festival?

What on earth would happen once they turned three?

It boggled the imagination.

To think Diana had once teased Paula mercilessly when she bemoaned the difficult existence of the housewife-mother. Little did she know. Her sister Paula was a saint.

Digging ditches was probably less exhausting than motherhood—and Diana was certain it paid a lot more, into the

bargain. But it was hard to imagine any job on earth with
dividends like the ones that came with parenthood.

Two days ago, as she strolled around the village of East
Hampton with the girls and Gregory Stewart, she'd had a
glimpse of what it could be like with a family of her own.
Once, in the ladies' auxiliary shop, an elderly woman had
commented upon how wonderfully well Diana's "husband"
took care of their children, and Diana had simply smiled and
not bothered to correct her. Foolish, yes, but for a few moments it had been very nice to pretend.

Today, however, she didn't have time to pretend. In the
next fifteen minutes her guests would begin to arrive, and she
had a score of details to check before the doorbell rang. She
swung open the refrigerator door and looked at the stacks of
containers crowding the shelves. Potato salad with onion and
hard-boiled egg; tomato and mozzarella vinaigrette with just
a hint of fresh basil from the farm stand in Amagansett; mac-
aroni salad, laced with a touch of honey; baked ham; fried
chicken; corn on the cob ready for the pot; and, of course,
hamburgers and hot dogs, all set to be grilled to perfection.

She'd been tempted to try out a cold broccoli, lemon and
garlic salad and a shrimp and bacon appetizer, but good sense
had at last prevailed. Mother had put her recipes away. As it
was, the assortment would be bountiful enough to make King
Henry VIII's mouth water. Until now, she hadn't exhibited
the slightest sign of competence in anything from child care
to driving to basic shopping skills. She owed it to herself to
redeem her good name.

"Oh, admit it," she said out loud as she closed the refrigerator door with a bang. "You want to knock the good doctor's socks off!"

She wanted Gregory Stewart to think she was the greatest
thing since color TV. Why else would she have spent an hour
fussing with her hair, when the warm, sea breeze would send
it curling around her face the second she stepped outside?
Why had she ironed her white cotton pants three times in
order to get the creases just right? Insanity, that was why.

Diana wasn't used to anything less than perfection, and the fact that the good doctor had seen her quite a few notches below her best bothered her more than she cared to admit.

And when the good doctor in question was young and strapping and magnificent to look at—well, it made the situation darn near intolerable.

Mother deserved better than that, and Diana was determined that she should get it.

She was about to race upstairs and change her red-and-white T-shirt for the blue one, when the front door chimes rang out. Her heart zigzagged against her rib cage, and her attempt to take a deep breath was not very successful.

She straightened her shoulders, mustered her best smile and opened the front door.

"Happy Fourth of July!" she beamed, all red, white and blue enthusiasm. "Welcome to Gull Cottage!"

"One more word out of you," said the receptionist, "and the barbecue is off!"

Chapter Eight

"I beg your pardon?" *I must be hallucinating. I don't even have a home to get sent to....* Diana stared openmouthed at the small red-haired woman, and wished she'd listened to her sister when Paula said, "Don't speak to strangers."

"I said we'll talk about it later, and I meant it."

"Aw, Ma-a-a!" Diana blinked and turned toward a short, skinny boy with a Yankee baseball cap pulled low over his forehead. "Just one, please? They're real little, and I'll do all the work, I promise. You'll never even know we got one in the house."

"Right," said the woman, "and when it's thirty degrees below zero and the snow is piling up, who's going to be out there? Me, that's who! Not on your life, Joey."

Suddenly Gregory Stewart appeared out of nowhere, carrying a huge case of soda. "Puppies," he said by way of greeting.

Diana's smile had trailed off into something she feared resembled a grimace. "Puppies?"

"Pros and cons. Our resident pet had herself a litter this morning."

"Oh." She felt a tug at the leg of her white pants, and looked down to see Kath smiling up at her, with lips and hands stained chocolate. *My pants,* she thought. *My beautiful, pristine white pants....*

"Puppies!" Kath's twin joined her. "Where puppies?"

"Gregory's dog had puppies," Diana told the girls.

"Where?"

"At his house," she said, praying the next question wasn't "Why?"

The red-haired woman crouched and stared solemnly at the twins. "I'm Mary Ann. Who are you?"

"Jennifer," said Kath.

"Kath-a-ryn," said Jenny.

"Reverse that," said Diana with a helpless shrug of her shoulders. "They like to play games with people."

"One of the benefits of being twins." The woman stood up and extended her hand to Diana. "I'm Mary Ann Marino, and I apologize for being rude."

Diana shook her hand. "Diana Travis, and no apology is necessary." She glanced at the young boy in the baseball cap. "Hi. And you're—?"

"Joey," he said, looking down at the twins as bright red color flooded his freckled cheeks. "Hello."

Gregory grinned at the group of them assembled on the front steps of Gull Cottage. "I should've introduced everyone, shouldn't I?"

"You clod," said Mary Ann. "And don't you dare blame it on lack of sleep. I'm just as tired as you are."

Whoa! thought Diana with a start, as some of her more elaborate fantasies began to crumble. Was there something between Mary Ann Marino and Gregory Stewart that she should know about?

Gregory met her eyes, and the message in his gaze was easy to understand. "She brought Joey over to watch Daisy deliver."

"Daisy?"

"The cocker spaniel."

Diana passed a hand across her forehead as an aged Volvo limped up the driveway and pulled under the porte cochere. "We have more company," she said as a man in his late twenties helped an extraordinarily pregnant woman from the

car. From the look of her, Diana wondered if she should start
boiling water.

"My partner Dave and his wife. She's due any day," said
Gregory.

"Really?" Diana murmured. "I hadn't noticed."

"Fat," said Jenny, pointing toward the woman walking
toward them.

"Fat as a cat," said Kath, as Ignatius the Huge ambled
out onto the front step.

Was it too late to back out of this barbecue?

BY TWO O'CLOCK, Diana had set up the trays of appetizers,
served drinks all around, made a second pitcher of fresh-
squeezed lemonade, changed the twins' diapers, arbitrated a
fight between Boris and Ignatius over ownership of the solarium, and decided she should retire upstairs to Cleopatra's
barge.

"What an idiot," she said to the empty kitchen as she
arranged fresh vegetables on her brand-new dinner plates. If
she had half a brain, she would grab the keys to the station
wagon and disappear until this particular debacle was over.

Not that anyone would notice, because they all seemed to
be having a wonderful time, eating and drinking and laughing
up a storm. They complimented her on the wonderful food
and the fabulous beverages and invited her to sit down and
join the party, but she felt as if she would explode if she
didn't keep moving. Simple conversation seemed beyond her
abilities; Boris would have been a more scintillating conver-
sationalist than Diana at that moment.

The twins were shamelessly flirting with Gregory, while
Mary Ann Marino and her son Joey played croquet on the
back lawn. Dave and his any-minute wife Peggy were sitting
by the pool, earnestly discussing whether they would send
their offspring to Harvard or Yale. No one seemed to notice,
when Diana excused herself, slipped into the house and went
upstairs to change her white pants for a pair of shorts.

If only her attitude could be changed just as easily....

Once downstairs again and in the kitchen, she grabbed a tiny paring knife to trim a leaf from a broccoli floret and nicked her index finger. "Oh, damn!" She popped her finger into her mouth. What an idiotic, ridiculous excuse for a household wizard she was. She couldn't even manage to trim vegetables without drawing blood.

She heard the sound of footsteps at the doorway, then Gregory's voice. "You okay?"

"Fine," she mumbled, keeping her head down. "I didn't think anyone knew I was gone." *Terrific. You sound like a petulant, five-year-old brat.*

"You don't sound fine." He started toward her.

"Go outside," she said, wiping her hand on a dish towel. "Enjoy the party."

"If you want me to enjoy the party, you'll let me stay inside."

"Big mistake," she said, attacking the innocent broccoli once again. "It's dangerous in here."

"Let me look at your hand."

She noted another drop of blood pooling near her fingertip. "Just a scratch."

"I'm a doctor," he said, reaching for her hand. "I have credentials."

"You're a vet," she said, meeting his eyes reluctantly. "Your credentials are only good for Boris and Iggy."

"We'll make an exception."

"Oh, why not?" She sighed deeply and leaned against the counter as he examined her finger. "The way today is going, you might as well perform an appendectomy, if you feel like it."

The antique wall clock that had somehow escaped the repo men chimed two o'clock. Somewhere on Long Island, at that very moment, her ex-husband and his pregnant cheerleader were saying "I do," when it was already painfully obvious that they already *had*.

Mazel tov!" she said under her breath.

He held her hand under the faucet and flushed the wound with warm water. "Thinking about the wedding?"

She flinched at the sting of soap. "How on earth do you know about the wedding?"

"You told me. Remember?" He patted her hand dry with a linen dish towel she'd bought at the pricey linen boutique on Main Street.

"You have an incredible memory." *And I have an incredibly big mouth.*

"Feel like talking about it?"

"What's to talk about? We were married. We were divorced. Jack's getting married again. Case closed."

His eyes were a gorgeous deep blue-green, and the expression in them was surprisingly tender. She looked away. She didn't know if she could handle tenderness.

"It's not what you think," she said after a moment. "I don't love him anymore, but I can't get his wedding out of my mind."

"Sounds normal to me."

"Depends on your definition of normal."

"I've been there before, Diana, and I felt the same way. The day Hayley got married, I drank myself into a stupor and tore up my apartment."

She forgot about her cut finger. "You've been married?"

"Engaged," he said, rummaging around in the drawer. "Don't you have any Band-Aids around here?"

"In the cabinet over the sink." She swiveled her head and watched him lean over to peer inside the cupboard. "Your fiancée married another man?"

He reached way back and extracted a tin. "Why don't you keep them where you can reach them?"

She ignored the criticism, mainly because he was right. Mother recommended keeping a full stocked first-aid kit in both kitchen and bathroom. "How long were you engaged?"

He leaned against the sink and, grabbing her wrist, drew her close so he could attend to her finger. "Two years, two and a half. We were living together. Taking the final step kept getting away from us. Guess our timing was off.''

''You have something against marriage?''

''I wouldn't know. I haven't tried it yet.'' He gave her a funny look from under his thick, dark brows. ''How about you?''

''I don't hold a grudge. Just because it didn't work the first time is no reason to give up on the institution, is it?''

He watched her carefully. ''If you want to call the party off, there'd be no hard feelings.''

''Right,'' she said, going back to the counter and her broccoli florets. ''I'm on shaky enough ground with Mary Ann. That's all I'd need. My name would be mud.''

''I told you the other morning it's nothing personal. Mary Ann's going through a tough time.''

''Her son?''

''How do you know?''

She neatly trimmed the leaves off a stalk. ''It wasn't hard to tell. Cancer?''

A small muscle in Gregory's throat moved convulsively before he spoke. ''Yes.''

''How bad is it?''

She heard the ragged intake of his breath, and her stomach knotted. ''Not that bad,'' Gregory said, but the expression in his eyes belied his words.

''He's so young.''

''Since when does being young protect you?''

She thought of Kath and Jenny, of their sunny smiles and beautiful faces, and wondered how it would feel to know their time was limited. ''Dear God,'' she whispered. ''How does Mary Ann manage?''

''She's a hell of a woman. She lives for that kid.''

''What about her husband, Joey's father?''

''He took off, just before she came to work for me.''

''He must come to see Joey. I mean, especially with him so—''

''Frank Marino doesn't want to know about any of it. He

has a new life, a new family—he doesn't have time for the kid.''

''The louse should be shot.''

''Mary Ann would be the first to agree with you.''

Diana cut into another stalk of broccoli. Not for her. She would find the right man this time, a man who wanted her for all the things she was—both good and not so good. She was old-fashioned enough to want the whole package, and stubborn enough to believe she could actually get it. She would find the right man, form a solid marriage. She'd waited a long time to have a child, and she was determined the father of that child would be as kind and honorable as—well, as the man standing before her seemed to be. Without that foundation, the rest was no more than castles in the air.

The kitchen door swung open, and Diana and Gregory turned to see Joey Marino, Yankee cap slipping to one side, standing in the doorway. ''Beach volleyball!'' he announced, his narrow face lighting up with his smile. ''Come on! We can't play without you.''

''What do you say?'' Gregory filched a piece of broccoli and popped it into his mouth.

The sweet sound of the girls' laughter floated in on the ocean breeze. The sky outside was deep blue; the sun, hot and bright. The refrigerator was stacked with delicious food and ice-cold lemonade and beer, and she was lucky enough to have a houseful of new friends to enjoy it.

''Please,'' said Joey with that winning smile. ''You can be on my team.''

The vision of her ex-husband and his pregnant girlfriend and their Independence Day wedding grew dimmer and dimmer, then finally disappeared.

''What the heck,'' Diana said, untying her apron and tossing it onto the countertop. ''Last one on the beach is a rotten egg.''

THEY WON the volleyball match, three games to one, and Diana knew full well that she hadn't contributed a heck of a lot to her team. From the moment Gregory stripped down to his swimming trunks, she was a goner. The sight of his broad, strong body clad in nothing more than a few scraps of cloth sent her temperature skyrocketing faster than the midday sun overhead.

So much for her imagination—his reality was far more impressive than anything her overheated mind had conjured up. Each time he leaped for a shot, muscles rippling, her mouth grew dry with something approaching terminal lust and she stood, rooted in place, while he did all the work— and she had all the fun.

Gregory was strong, fast, and devious and their opponents—Mary Ann, Dave and Joey—didn't stand a chance against him.

"Another match?" Gregory challenged, tossing the ball to Joey.

"Forget it," said Dave, collapsing on the sand next to Peggy, who'd been playing with the twins. "I'm dead."

"I'm going back to the house and diving into the pool," said Mary Ann, wiping sweat from her forehead with the back of her hand. "I may even eat dinner in the pool."

Joey twirled the volleyball on the tip of one index finger. "Ma, can I—?"

Mary Ann grabbed the volleyball and lobbed it back to Gregory. "No, you can't," she said. "Remember the buddy system? I need someone around, in case I fall asleep in the middle of the pool."

Gregory turned to Diana. "Would you like to—?"

"Forget it! Being on your team is one thing. Playing against you is something else."

"I was going to ask if you wanted to take a walk up the beach with me."

"What about the twins?"

"Don't worry about them," said Peggy. "Dave and I need the practice."

Diana hesitated. "I don't know if—"

"Go ahead," said Dave. "We might as well see what's ahead of us two years down the road."

Apparently that was enough for Gregory, because he took Diana by the elbow and propelled her down toward the water and away from his friends.

"I didn't say yes yet," Diana said as she fell into step with him.

"You were going to."

"You didn't give me a chance."

"Who has time to wait?" he countered. "This might be the last chance I have all day to get you alone."

A delicious shiver raced up her spine, despite the hot sun on her back and the warm water lapping about her ankles. "We're hardly alone," she said, gesturing toward the crowds of people sunning and swimming up and down the beach.

"Damn shame," said Gregory, draping an arm casually about her shoulder.

Okay, she thought as they strolled along the water's edge. *It's a friendly gesture. Don't go reading anything else into it.* Just because she'd been out of the mainstream for a while was no reason to start hyperventilating like a love-struck maiden, was it? She cast about for a safe, nonsexual topic of conversation. "You're a terrific volleyball player," she offered. "Where'd you learn?"

"California," he said. "You don't grow up on the beaches and not learn to play a decent game of volleyball."

"I suppose you surf, too?"

"Guilty. I'm a member of Beach Boys Anonymous."

"The East Coast must have come as a shock to your system."

"Only the weather," he said, steering her around a large and wicked-looking jellyfish that was spread across a spray of seaweed. "It took me three years to discover winter has compensations."

"Let me guess: you learned to ski."

He laughed and drew her closer, until the heat of his skin burned through the thin cotton of her T-shirt. "There's no substitute for getting physical," he said. "At least none worth talking about."

"I spent six months in California after my divorce. If I never see another surfboard again, it'll be too soon."

"Not the outdoor type?"

She gave him a look. "Not exactly."

His smile was wicked. "Indoor sports aren't bad."

"No," she said, "I suppose they're not." She'd seen how he handled the outdoor variety; she could only dream about how he would handle the indoor. *Time to change the subject again.* "My ex-husband is an intellectual who didn't believe in expending any more energy than necessary. Going out for the Sunday paper was enough exercise for both of us."

Gregory's eyebrows lifted. "He's marrying a pregnant cheerleader—he must have expended some energy with her."

"Male menopause," Diana said dryly. "It happens to the best of your gender."

"That why he left?"

"He didn't leave, Gregory. It was a mutual decision."

"You can tell me it's none of my business."

"It *is* none of your business, but I don't mind telling you. He wanted kids. I didn't. Simple as that."

"Any regrets?"

She was silent for a moment as they passed a group of toddlers, playing at the water's edge under the eagle-eyed supervision of three young women in maternity swimsuits. "The time wasn't right for me then."

"What about now?"

"The time's right," she said with a rueful laugh. "Unfortunately, I no longer have a husband." She thought about telling him of her Great Labor Day Husband Hunt, but thought better of it. She'd only be in East Hampton for the month; why scare the man off?

"Bad timing's probably killed more relationships than infidelity," he said.

She thought about what he'd told her earlier about his fiancée. "Then I guess we have something in common."

He stopped abruptly. "You mean, besides this?"

Before she knew what had hit her, she was in his arms, and his mouth was covering hers in a kiss as breathtakingly sexual as it was sweet. Unfortunately by the time she recovered from the surprise, he had broken the kiss and brushed a lock of hair away from her mouth with a proprietary tenderness that was nearly her undoing.

"Why did you—?"

He touched her lips with a forefinger. "Because the timing was right."

"Yes," said Diana, her voice soft with pleasure. "I guess it was, at that."

IF GREGORY HAD HAD HIS WAY, that kiss would have led into other, more intense pleasures. However, the beach was crowded with Fourth of July revelers—and back at Gull Cottage, a number of nosy friends awaited his return.

The timing might have been right, but it sure hadn't been perfect, so it was with great reluctance that he led Diana back to the party.

Peggy and Dave were still sitting on the sand with the twins, and Diana stopped to admire the sand castle the little girls were laboriously constructing with more enthusiasm than skill. His gaze lingered on the curve of her breasts as she crouched near the sand castle, and he quickly glanced away as he caught Dave and Peggy exchanging amused looks.

"Want me to start the barbecue?" he asked Diana.

"Terrific," she said, looking at him, her eyes wide and lovely. "I'd appreciate it."

He turned and headed toward the beach steps, positive he'd only have to look at the coals and they'd start burning.

Mary Ann was drifting quietly on an inflatable raft. Her eyes were closed, and he wasn't about to announce his arrival and face her intense—and nosy—questioning about his relationship with Diana.

What relationship? Gregory thought as he piled charcoal

into the barbecue grill. With Diana due to leave Gull Cottage at the end of the month and himself prepared to leave East Hampton by August 15, the best they could manage would be a short-lived, summer romance. Unfortunately, he had the distinct feeling that short-lived, summer romances weren't what Diana Travis was all about. The look of permanence was all over her lovely face, and that was the one thing he couldn't offer.

So why then was he finding it so damned hard to pull away?

Gregory had no answer to that question—or to a number of others that were plaguing him—so he turned his full attention to the matter at hand: getting the barbecue started.

Maybe it was the call of some distant ancestor, but there was something downright atavistic about his attraction to fire in general and to barbecue grills in particular. Granted, trekking off to the wilds of the A and P meat counter for burgers and franks wasn't exactly like clubbing Bigfoot and dragging him back to camp, but it satisfied some deeply rooted need for male rituals that Phil Donahue had somehow forgotten to explore.

Laughter rang out from the staircase leading up from the beach, and he turned to see Diana, face flushed and smiling as the twins danced around her legs, hold out her hand to help Joey up the last few steps. Even in the uncompromising sunshine she looked lovely and hopeful and so deeply, innately maternal that something inside his chest twisted with pain. He averted his gaze.

"Cow eyes," murmured a suddenly vigilant Mary Ann from the swimming pool.

"Shut up," muttered Greg, brandishing the serving fork in her direction, "or I'll puncture your float."

Diana, Joey and the twins strolled over to the barbecue.

"Where's Dave and Peggy?" Gregory asked. "Don't tell me she's having false labor again?"

Diana laughed and steered the girls away from the grill. "I don't know whether it's false labor or not, but she's not

feeling too hot. Dave's walking her along the shore to see i[.
the discomfort passes.''

"It'll pass," said Gregory with a shake of his head. "Tha
baby's going to hang on as long as possible."

"I have a feeling today's the day," Diana said.

"The baby hasn't dropped yet," Mary Ann offered from
the middle of the swimming pool. "She still has a while to
go."

"Today," Diana repeated. "I have a sixth sense about
these things."

"Do you have any kids?"

"No, but—"

"Talk to me after you've gone through labor yourself,"
Mary Ann said. "Believe me, it isn't her time yet."

"It is," said Diana. "Mark my words."

Gregory busied himself at the barbecue in an attempt to
hide the grin on his face. Few people stood up to the opinionated Mary Ann Marino, and it was fun to see his receptionist set down a peg or two.

"Another five minutes and the coals will be red-hot," he
announced. "You can start cooking anytime."

"Terrific," said Diana, taking her nieces by the hand.
"We'll bring out the burgers and franks."

Joey cleared his throat. Patches of scarlet colored his
sunken cheeks. "Can I help?"

Diana glanced at Mary Ann, who nodded slightly, then
favored the boy with a dazzling smile. "Come on, Joey,"
she said, her voice warm and friendly. "I could use a strong
pair of arms to carry things out."

Joey trailed into the house after Diana. Gregory could almost hear the sound of violins in the air.

Smart kid.

THERE WAS SOMETHING about sitting around a picnic table
with a woman nine months and two weeks pregnant that had
an odd effect on conversation.

Peggy's discomfort hadn't let up. Twice during the salads

she'd risen to her feet, and they'd all held their collective breath, waiting for the announcement that it was time to go to the hospital. Both times Peggy had shrugged in defeat, then sat down again to enjoy the feast, while poor Dave grew older before their eyes.

"I think we should start a betting pool," Gregory said as he served up the giant-sized hamburgers and foot-long hot dogs. "I say July 11th."

"The ninth," said Mary Ann.

"2001," said the beleaguered Dave, to everyone's amusement.

"Today," said Diana, winking at Peggy.

"Ridiculous," said Gregory, handing her a cheeseburger supreme with the works. "You haven't gone through three false alarms. I'm telling you, she isn't even close."

"Believe me, I know when a woman is due," said Mary Ann, suddenly the loyal employee, "and Peggy isn't close yet. I had one of my own and watched my four sisters through eleven pregnancies. The twelfth, at the earliest."

"Before midnight," Diana said calmly.

"Forget it," said Gregory.

"That's crazy," said Mary Ann.

"I'll never become a father," said Dave.

"I think it's time," said Peggy.

The only sound was the crunch of corn on the cob being devoured by Joey and the curly-haired twins.

"Very funny," said Dave after a long and uneasy silence. "You've made your point. A betting pool was a pretty tacky idea."

"I'm serious, Davey. It's time."

"How far apart are the pains?" Diana asked, putting down her plate at the edge of the swimming pool and approaching Peggy.

"Seven minutes and—" Peggy stopped, and Gregory watched, horrified, as her eyes closed and her face contorted with pain. This was a far cry from watching Daisy deliver her pups, and he suddenly felt foolish and unnecessary in the face of such pure drama.

"Ride it out," Diana instructed Peggy, all business. "Time the contractions," she ordered Dave.

"This has happened before," Dave said, fumbling through his pockets for his stopwatch. "This can't be the real thing."

"It's the real thing," Diana said as Peggy rode out another contraction. "Her water just broke."

"Oh, my God," said Dave, sinking back into his chair, a wretched shell of the man he'd once been. "We're going to have a baby."

Chapter Nine

Twenty minutes later they were once again gathered on the patio, eating their delayed supper. Mary Ann had pulled the float from the swimming pool and was now using it as an inflatable cushion. Joey sat at the edge of the pool, his feet dangling in the water. The twins were seated at their own little table that Gregory had carted out from the kitchen, to their squeals of delight. The good doctor himself, however, was seated on the ground next to the barbecue with plates of food balanced on his powerful thighs.

Diana had a wonderful view of said thighs, for she was sitting on the back step, midway between the twins and the barbecue, and she didn't know which was the more delicious: her tomato-and-mozzarella salad or Gregory Stewart. Mary Ann and Gregory were involved in a lively debate on the relative merits of the New York Yankees and the New York Mets, while Diana merely nodded and feasted on the sight of his beautifully muscular body in repose.

It took Joey to bring them back to the topic that was—or should have been—on everybody's mind.

"How long does it take to have a baby?" he piped up, reaching for an ear of roasted corn.

"Depends," said Mary Ann. "Your Aunt Susie had Denise by the time Uncle Frankie backed the car out of the garage."

"My father would have loved that," said Diana. "Talk about efficiency."

Gregory laughed and passed Joey the salt and pepper. "How about you, M.A.? How long did this guy here keep you waiting?"

Mary Ann groaned and covered her face with her hands. "Twenty-seven hours, eighteen minutes and forty-five seconds—not that I was counting, you understand."

Diana winced in sympathy. "You're a brave woman, Mary Ann."

Mary Ann gave Diana her first real smile of the day. "Bravery had nothing to do with it. If I'd had my way, I would have grabbed my bathrobe and headed for the hills."

"Hey, Ma!" Joey looked up from his food. "You said it was worth the trouble."

"Oh, yeah?" Mary Ann winked at Diana and Gregory. "Do you have it in writing?" She tempered her words with a tug at the bill of Joey's Yankee cap.

"Can I eat my burger on the beach steps?" Joey asked, grabbing another pickle from the bowl set out on the girls' table.

Mary Ann considered his request. "You won't disappear on me, like you did at your cousin's Memorial Day party?"

He shook his head vigorously. "I promise. Just the steps, only halfway down."

"All right," Mary Ann said, "but your bottom better stay in contact with those stairs or you're in trouble, mister."

"Aw-right!" With a grin Joey leaped to his feet, then headed across the backyard toward the beach steps, carrying a plate of food and a can of Pepsi.

"Me! Me!" cried the twins, eager to follow their brand-new friend. "Beach!"

"Not this time," said Diana. "You stay here with the grown-ups."

"No!" cried Jenny, stomping one bare foot hard on the tiles around the pool. "Me too!"

"Sorry, honey. I said no."

"Yes!" Kath pushed out her lower lip defiantly in imitation of her twin. "Yes!"

The one thing Diana wanted to avoid was being tricked into a debate with a pair of cranky two-year-olds. The possibility of losing the battle was too humiliating to even consider.

"Why don't you finish your supper?" she coaxed. "Later on we'll have watermelon." Not above bribery, she popped a perfect red cherry tomato onto each of their plates, while they eyed their food with outraged suspicion.

"Don't like." Kath pushed the tomato around with one finger. "Bad!"

Jenny spit a piece of hot dog onto her plate. "Bad!"

Then, as if on cue, the two began to cry at the top of their toddlers' lungs.

"What did I do?" Diana looked over at Mary Ann, who'd been watching the whole thing with an air of maternal amusement. "Is this what they mean by the terrible twos?"

"At least you get to give them back when the month is up."

"I've never seen them like this," Diana said as both girls tipped their paper plates onto their laps and shrieked even louder. "It's like Jekyll and Hyde in duplicate."

"Welcome to the wide world of motherhood," Mary Ann said as Gregory—the traitor—beat a hasty retreat toward the beach steps and male companionship. "Maybe they need changing."

"They're pretty good about letting me know what they want. They used the potty just before Dave and Peggy left."

"You'd be surprised how quickly toilet training can go out the window." Mary Ann put down her plate of food, then scooped the squalling Kath into her arms to check the diaper. "Bingo. She needs changing."

Diana picked up a kicking Jenny and struggled to do the same. "I can't believe it. So does she." She grimaced at the streaks of ketchup staining the child's T-shirt. "In fact, they need changing from the inside out. They look like they were rolling around in a condiment tray.'' Rising to her feet, she held out her hand for Kath. ''Come on, girls. We have a little work ahead of us.''

Mary Ann stood up with Kath still in her arms. ''I'll help you.''

''No—I mean, that's very nice of you, but you're a guest. The last thing you need is diaper duty.''

''I'd enjoy it.''

Diana arched a brow. ''You don't expect me to believe that, do you?''

''Really,'' said Mary Ann with an embarrassed laugh. ''I'd love to fuss over a little girl.'' She hesitated, then met Diana's eyes. ''That is, if you don't mind.''

''I'd welcome some expert help. Come on,'' she said as she hoisted Jenny into her arms. ''We're short on furniture inside but long on diapers.''

Mary Ann rolled her eyes heavenward. ''The story of my life.''

Diana led the way up the back staircase to the master bedroom. ''The main bathroom is through here,'' she said, tossing the words over her shoulder as she switched on the light. ''It's a double vanity. We'll just—'' She stopped in midsentence as she realized that Mary Ann, with Kath in her arms, was rooted to the middle of the floor.

''My God!'' the red-haired woman breathed. ''Tell me I'm hallucinating.''

''You're not hallucinating.''

''Is that a bed or a high-rise apartment?''

''It's a bed,'' Diana said, grinning at the expression on Mary Ann's freckled face. ''Pretty incredible, isn't it?''

Mary Ann approached the swagged and gilt-trimmed bed with the caution usually saved for midnight trips to darkened basements. She jiggled the ladder leading up to the monster mattress. ''Do you get nosebleeds up there?''

''Not yet, but thank God I'm not afraid of heights.''

The slot machine in the bathroom made Mary Ann roar with laughter, and before long even the twins had been jollied out of their temper tantrums and were soon giggling right along with the two women.

"I like your style," said Mary Ann, as Diana fastened a diaper around Jenny's chubby bottom. "You're a downright natural at diaper duty."

Diana inclined her head graciously. "I'll take that as a compliment."

"I meant it as one." Mary Ann patted baby powder onto Kath's rear, then fixed the diaper in place. "Any plans on having one of your own?"

"Detailed plans. All beginning Labor Day."

Mary Ann's gaze drifted toward Diana's middle, then hurriedly bounced up to meet her eyes. "You're pregnant?"

"Not yet, but I will be."

"On Labor Day?"

"In a way. Starting on Labor Day, I'm plunging back into the dating world, with a goal of marriage by New Year's Eve."

Mary Ann deftly pulled a pair of bright yellow overalls onto Kath's wiggling body. "Do you always set deadlines for yourself?"

"I *live* for deadlines," Diana said, struggling to get Jenny's legs into her apple-red pants. "I intend to be married by this time next year." *And maybe pregnant.*

"You're kidding!" Mary Ann looked at Diana curiously. "You *are* kidding, aren't you?"

"You sound just like my sister Paula did when I told her." She tucked Jenny's clean T-shirt into the elastic waistband of the pants.

"You're crazy. Nobody can plan things like that."

"I found my first husband pretty easily. I should be able to find another without too much trouble."

"Good luck," Mary Ann said, smoothing Kath's curls off the toddler's forehead. "It's a cold, cold world out there, and good men are at a premium."

"I know," Diana said, undeterred by the other woman's

pessimism. "But I believe the right one's out there, and I'm going to find him."

"Optimists," said Mary Ann, with a rueful shake of her head. "Your type amazes me. Didn't anyone ever tell you that you don't get everything you want in life?"

"A little positive thinking never hurt anyone," Diana offered gently.

"Let me tell you, it's easier on the heart to join a convent."

Diana gestured toward the twins, who were making faces at each other in the vanity mirror. "Quite a compensation for risking your heart."

Mary Ann nodded, but Diana could see the skepticism in her blue eyes.

"You don't know the half of it," her new friend said softly.

Impulsively Diana reached over and patted Mary Ann's forearm. "Joey's a great kid. You should be very proud of him."

"You do know he has a major league-sized crush on you, don't you?"

"I suspected as much."

"I hope he didn't make a pest of himself down on the beach."

"He's a dear," Diana said. "Clever and funny and very sweet." She wanted to acknowledge that she knew about Joey's illness, but the words wouldn't come.

"Kids," said Mary Ann as Kath wrapped her arms around her neck and planted a noisy kiss upon her cheek. "Heartbreak, pain, and a permanent drain on your bank balance. Change your mind, while there's still time."

Jenny, not to be outdone by her sister, threw herself into Diana's arms and gave her a wet and sloppy kiss on the chin. Her already sentimental heart turned to mush.

"Just tell me one thing," she said, meeting Mary Ann's gaze. "Would you do it all again?"

Mary Ann considered the question for an endless moment.

"Yes," she said at last, "I believe I would. Even knowing. I wouldn't have missed Joey for the world."

Diana shivered, as a glimpse of reality crowded in on her dream. *I'll be one of the lucky ones,* she vowed silently as they finished dressing her nieces. Her whole life had been blessed by the hand of Lady Luck. Even her divorce had been *her* decision, a result of *her* desire for a career and not a child. She'd been wrong to think it an either-or proposition. Everywhere she looked, women were combining marriage and career. Everywhere she looked, women her age and older were having babies. She had to trust that Lady Luck, in her infinite variety, wouldn't fail her now.

"You know," said Mary Ann, "I didn't think I would like you, but I do."

"I *knew* I didn't like you," said Diana, "but I was wrong."

Mary Ann gestured toward the opulent Gull Cottage surroundings and sighed wistfully. "You have everything I always wanted: success, money, great legs. I'm green with envy."

"Don't be," said Diana, pressing a kiss atop Jenny's curly, blond hair. "You have Joey. That's better than anything I can think of."

GREGORY AND JOEY sat on the bottom step, watching the setting sun turn the Atlantic into liquid flame. Farther down the beach, a camp fire glowed red in the gathering darkness, and the scent of hickory mingled with the tang of salt in the air. A few sea gulls stood sentinel along the shoreline, and every now and again one would follow the tide back out in search of food. At a moment like this it was easy to forget the clog of humanity that weighed down the Hamptons every summer, filling the country air with the smell of exhaust and the sound of city talk, city problems and city dreams.

"How long does it take to change diapers?" Joey asked, picking up a small rock and flinging it toward the ocean a few hundred yards away. "They've been gone a long time."

Gregory peered at his watch in the dusky light. "Not that long, pal. My company's not good enough for you anymore?"

Joey looked down at his bare toes peeking out from the heavy, damp sand. "I thought they'd be back sooner than this."

"Miss your mom, do you?"

The boy shrugged noncommittally.

Gregory grinned. "Why is it I think you kind of miss Diana?" Who could blame the kid? Gregory missed her himself, and she'd only been gone fifteen minutes.

"She's okay." Joey continued to search through the sand for rocks to toss.

"Nothing wrong with thinking a lady is okay."

"You better not tell anybody."

"Who, me? You know better than that, pal. It's our secret." *Along with the fact that I find her pretty okay myself....*

The boy turned and looked over at Gregory. "Do you think she likes me?"

"What's not to like?" Gregory countered, tugging at the bill of Joey's baseball cap. "You're a good kid."

"I don't want to be a kid."

"Afraid you don't have much choice for the moment."

"Being a kid stinks."

"Don't worry. It doesn't last forever. You'll be paying taxes soon enough."

Laughter floated toward them from up the beach, tinkling like the wind chimes that hung over the patio.

"Do you like my mom?" Joey asked.

Strange question. "Very much." He waited a beat, then: "Why do you ask?"

"You know what I mean," the boy persisted. "Do you *like* her?"

"You mean the way a man likes a woman?"

"Yeah," Joey mumbled. "More than the way you like a friend."

Why tonight, Joey? Couldn't you pick another night for

this? He wanted to think about Diana, think about the way the sunlight sparkled on her golden hair, think about the sweet inward curve of her waist and the long and luscious length of leg exposed by her shorts.

"Do you like her that way?" Joey resumed.

"I love your mom as a friend, pal, but not as a girlfriend. Do you understand what I mean?"

The boy shrugged his thin shoulders. "I guess."

He had respect and admiration and a deep, abiding affection for Mary Ann, but nowhere in that mixture was the intangible chemical reaction that made the difference between the sexes infinitely appealing—the chemical reaction that had been there for him the first moment he laid eyes on Diana. "What made you ask?"

Joey was his mother's son, and his answer was as direct as one of Mary Ann's barbs. "I thought if you married my mom, you could stay here."

"You mean, not go away?"

"Yeah...something like that."

He draped an arm around the boy, feeling the bones so plainly beneath the skin. "I'm not going away forever, you know. Do you think I'd let Dave and Charlie take over the hospital? They'd have Daisy and her pups running the place. I'll be back by Christmas."

"That's a long time from now."

"Not when you get to be my age, it's not."

"It is when you're my age," Joey retorted.

"I have to go, Joey. You understand, don't you?"

Joey said nothing, his lower lip set in a stubborn position.

"I've waited a long time, kid. I owe it to myself." He fought down a wave of pure, unadulterated sentimentality. "One day you'll understand."

"No, I won't," said Joey. "I think you're running away."

"You're right," said Gregory. "That's exactly what I'm going to do, and if you're my friend, you'll try to understand."

Joey turned and met Gregory's eyes. "I'm your friend," he said slowly, "but I don't think I'm gonna understand."

"Will you give it a try?"

"Yeah," muttered Joey. "But I'm not making any promises."

"Deal?" Gregory extended his hand.

"Deal." Joey picked up a stone and tossed it toward the water. "Greg?"

"What, Joey?"

"I still say it stinks."

Gregory's laughter melted into the night air. "So do I, kid," he said after a pause. "At the moment, so do I."

Chapter Ten

"I thought they'd never leave," Gregory said as Mary Ann's Hyundai disappeared around a bend in the driveway a few hours later. "I hate people who wear out their welcome."

How on earth had it happened? Diana had gone inside to make coffee, and when she came back onto the patio, the Marinos were ready to leave.

Diana wheeled and headed toward the house. "I don't understand it." She glanced over her shoulder as she crossed the foyer with him hard on her heels. "You must have done something to offend them."

"What's that supposed to mean?"

"I couldn't get Joey to stay for dessert. Twelve-year-old boys would *kill* for dessert."

"It was getting late."

"You didn't suggest they head for home?"

"Why are you so suspicious?"

"I've learned a lot about you in the past few days, Gregory. You're many things, but subtle isn't among them."

"My approach isn't subtle, but you have to admit I get results."

"A bullwhip gets results, too, but it's not socially acceptable."

She pushed past him into the huge solarium and made a show of checking on the girls, who were sleeping in front of the television set, on the cat, who was sleeping on top of the set, and on the mynah bird who sat, laughing at them all, from the safety of his cage. She adjusted the transmitter on the baby monitor she'd purchased in town yesterday. She would do anything rather than face up to the fact that she was alone with him and scared to death. "If you had any decency, you'd say good-night."

"I haven't had my coffee yet."

"I'm sure there's a diner open someplace."

He flipped her a fifty-cent piece that she caught neatly in her right hand. "Think that'll get me a cup of coffee and some of that chocolate cheesecake I saw in the refrigerator?"

"It might." The coin was warm from his body, and she clutched it in the palm of her hand as a rush of odd sensations flooded through her. This was what she'd been trying to avoid all day, ever since their interludes in the kitchen and on the beach. Gregory Stewart had the unnerving ability to cut through her defenses. Already he knew more about the workings of her heart than most of her friends ever would. "Come on," she said, tossing the half dollar back to him. "You took care of the barbecue. I suppose the least I can do is give you that cup of coffee."

He pocketed the coin, then draped an arm lightly around her shoulders. "I was hoping you'd see it my way."

You're out of practice, girl, she thought as they strolled down the hallway to the kitchen in the rear of the house. This was not a sexual situation. This wasn't even a date. Dates didn't include twin toddlers, fat cats, loud-mouthed mynahs and divorced mothers with big-eyed sons who tore at your heartstrings.

Just because he'd kissed her on the beach that afternoon was no reason to think he had any intention of kissing her again. As he'd said, the timing then had been right; it was as simple as that.

Dates included two people, at least one of whom had romance on his or her mind.

Gregory drew her closer as they entered the darkened kitchen, and her pulses quickened alarmingly.

Like now?

She slipped out of his grasp and switched on the overhead light. There was nothing like fluorescent lighting to point out a person's weak spots. Unfortunately, he didn't have any.

"This really isn't fair," she muttered to herself, certain her own facial flaws were standing out in bas-relief. "Were you airbrushed at birth?"

His thick, dark brows slid together. "What was that?"

"I said, do you use cream or do you take your coffee black?"

"Black," he said, "and no, I wasn't airbrushed."

She nearly dropped the coffeepot onto the tile floor. "You louse! You heard what I said."

"Every word."

"You can go home now, Dr. Stewart. My humiliation is officially complete."

"You did say it out loud, didn't you? Why are you so surprised I heard it?"

She sighed deeply and put the coffeepot down. "This pathetic wretch you see before you is the result of what happens to a once-normal woman, after she's spent three years alone with a cat."

"You talk to Ignatius?"

"You probably think that's weird."

"Only if you tell me he talks back to you."

"Not yet, but after a month with Boris, who knows?"

"Call me if he starts meowing the Gettysburg Address. We'll make a million."

She poured the coffee, then cut them each a wedge of the cheesecake. They took their dessert out to the patio and sat at the edge of the swimming pool with the receiver of the baby monitor not far away. The glow from the citronella candles was reflected in the still water. Dusk had finally given way to darkness, and the sky was a swathe of black velvet, dotted with a haze of diamonds and blurred by a thin wash of clouds.

The easy, companionable feeling of the early part of the

evening was gone, and in its place was a heightened—almost painful—awareness of his nearness. He ate with an economy of motion, but each time he lifted the fork to his mouth, his body rippled with muscles most men didn't even have.

What an idiotic notion! Gregory Stewart had the standard issue male body; it was just packaged better than most, that was all. There was certainly no mystery to that.

And she happened to enjoy looking at it.

There was certainly no mystery to that, either.

Show her a woman who didn't appreciate a beautiful pair of biceps, and she'd show you a woman without a soul....

Be honest, Mother, her conscience prodded. *It isn't your soul that's on Red Alert.*

"Coffee's good," he said.

"Thanks."

"Cheesecake's good, too."

"Thank the bakery for that. You were with me when I got it."

"Are you back on that I-give-lousy-parties routine again?"

"Take a look around you, Dr. Stewart. It's eight o'clock, and you're the only one left."

"So?"

"What do you mean 'so'? I lose party guests quicker than Sean Penn loses his temper."

He leaned back on his elbows and looked up at her. Even by candlelight he looked terrific. That thought depressed her even more.

"I told Mary Ann to leave."

"You *what*?"

"I told Mary Ann to leave, while you were on the phone the second time with your sister."

Diana leaped to her feet. "Get out."

"Aren't you overreacting?"

"Get out, before I throw you out!"

"Mother wouldn't treat a guest like that."

"Party's over, Dr. Stewart," she said, chest heaving with

outrage, ''and you're not a guest anymore. You're a tres-
passer.''

''You have no sense of humor, Diana. Anyone ever tell
you that?''

''My ex-husband. You're in wonderful company.''

She turned, about to storm back into the house, but he
caught her around the ankle, and she fell backward across
his lap with a yelp of surprise.

''Are you hurt?'' His face was so close that she caught the
aroma of coffee on his breath and the tang of salt air on his
skin.

''Only my dignity.'' She tried to pull away, but he held
her fast. All day she'd been imagining how it would feel to
be in his arms—and now that she was, she wanted nothing
more than to escape. ''Let me go!'' If only she sounded as
if she meant it.

''Not yet.'' His hand slid up her calf, caressing the tensed
knot of muscle, then easing along the sensitive hollow behind
her knee. ''I've wanted to do this for hours.'' She made a
sound of protest, but words were beyond her ability.

He stroked the back of her knee with the pads of his fingers, while his palm pressed warmly against the muscle of
her thigh. ''In fact, I waited all afternoon for you to strip
down to your swimsuit.''

Her power of speech returned at the thought of displaying
her thighs to his fevered gaze. ''I wondered why you made
such a production of going in the pool. You did everything
but send up fireworks.''

His hand inched higher up her thigh. ''What do you have
on under those shorts? A string bikini?''

Desire flared hotter at the thought of his fingers splayed
across the naked flesh of her hip. ''No string bikini,'' she
managed. ''Ten pounds ago maybe, but not now.''

His other hand stroked her back in lazy, honeyed circles
that made it hard for her to think. ''You look great to me.''

''You're a kind man.''

''No, I'm not. I'm blunt and opinionated and innately selfish, and I don't do or say anything I don't mean. You're sexy as hell, Diana.''

''I don't know what to say.''

''Why say anything?'' He lowered his face toward hers.

''This is crazy,'' she murmured, her hands pressed against the muscular wall of his chest. ''I—''

''Shut up, Diana,'' he said, his voice as dark as the night and infinitely exciting. ''Shut up and let me kiss you.''

Yes.... He closed the distance between them, capturing the sound until she wasn't certain if she had spoken at all or merely imagined it. His mouth was demanding against hers, the kiss powerful and urgent. His tongue moved tantalizingly across her lower lip, and she parted her lips slightly and gasped as he coaxed her tongue into sensual battle, deepening the kiss until even the sound of their breathing in the sheltering, summer darkness became erotic to her ears.

How long had it been since a simple kiss had the power to send her mind spiraling up and out of her body until she felt as if her consciousness was drifting somewhere above the stars? Ten years? Twenty?

Why, she could almost swear she heard fireworks.

And the telephone.

''Let it ring,'' he murmured, breaking the kiss for an instant.

Diana needed no coaxing. She clasped her hands lightly around his neck and brought his mouth to hers again.

The phone rang a second time, and then a third.

''Persistent.'' Gregory kissed the side of her neck. ''Probably your sister.''

''Mmm.'' Diana closed her eyes and drifted on a sea of exquisite sensation. *Go away, Paula. Leave me alone.*

The phone fell silent. The only sounds were those of the ocean crashing against the shore and the syncopated pounding of her heart. It was the first time in Diana's life that her sister had ever listened to her.

Talk about perfect timing.

How delightful it was to discover that the amazing Dr

Stewart kissed as well as he looked—which was really saying something, since he was easily the most gorgeous collection of male hormones Diana had ever seen.

Grasping her by the waist, he repositioned her so that she was curled toward him; her breasts were flattened against his chest, the snap on his jeans bit into the slight curve of her belly. Intimate, tantalizing contact made all the more shockingly wonderful by the sheer surprise of it all.

And once again the phone rang.

"You need an answering machine."

Her sense of responsibility reared its ugly head. "It might be important. Maybe I should answer it this time."

"It must be three in the morning in Monte Carlo. Doesn't your sister ever sleep?"

"It might be Dave." She struggled to her feet, leaning against his shoulder for balance.

"I doubt it. I don't think that baby's coming before Thanksgiving."

The ringing of the telephone continued, and she started toward the back door. "There's only one way to find out."

He rose and followed her, muttering something about leaving the receiver off the hook next time. Suddenly she felt self-conscious, acutely aware of the sway of her hips, the slight jiggle of her breasts beneath her T-shirt, of his gaze upon her and the fact that she'd give anything to be five foot eight of willowy elegance.

An answering machine, she thought, dashing across the kitchen toward the wall phone. An answering machine that gave an hourly report on the health and welfare of the twins, complete with EKG and resting pulse rate. Anything to tame Paula's mad urge to call at the drop of a franc.

But this time it wasn't Paula at all.

It was Dave, announcing the birth of a strapping, seven pound, eight ounce boy who, according to the proud new father, had "Peggy's eyes and my lung power."

She handed the telephone to Gregory, so that he could hear the details directly from his partner, while she rooted around in the newly stocked refrigerator for something celebratory to toast the occasion. Mother would have to remind her readers of the importance of having a bottle of champagne on hand at all times for times such as this.

"It's not Taittinger's," she said as she handed Gregory an icy bottle of Bud Lite, "but the sentiment is the same."

He grinned and took the bottle from her. "Still think you give lousy parties?"

"As a matter of fact, I'm thinking of claiming full credit for this blessed event."

"To new life." He raised his bottle high.

"To new life." She clinked her bottle against his, then they linked arms and drank.

From somewhere up the beach came the sharp crack of fireworks, and they turned to the window, in time to see the flash of a rocket exploding over the water. A sudden rush of emotion overtook Diana, and the tears she'd withheld all day rolled freely down her cheeks. She stared straight ahead at the makeshift fireworks display and made no attempt to brush the tears away lest she draw attention to them, but Gregory draped an arm across her shoulders and drew her close to his side.

All day long she had lived at the outer edge of her emotions, swept up by strong currents of yearning for the things she'd spent a lifetime postponing for the future. That afternoon, right there at Gull Cottage, the entire spectrum had been displayed before her: Peggy, ripe with child, at the beginning of that incredible journey; the twins, beautiful and bubbly, Paula's miraculous achievement. And Joey, so brave and so painfully young.

Mary Ann Marino had called her an optimist, but Diana didn't know if it was optimism or stupidity that made her so certain she would never know the darker side of life. Not even her divorce had seemed traumatic. Bad timing, not bad blood, had brought an end to their marriage, and she carried no scars or bruises like the ones Mary Ann bore.

She worked too much and she ate too much and she moved

from place to place like a gypsy, but it was all her choice. She scheduled her life because she liked schedules, because she liked to make her own decisions and know what was going to happen each morning before she opened her eyes.

And so far it had worked. She was where she wanted to be, when she wanted to be there.

In an uncertain world that was something, indeed.

Lucky, she thought, shivering slightly. *Lucky, lucky girl....*

"Cold?" he asked.

She shook her head. "I'm fine."

"Been a hell of a day, hasn't it?"

"Oh, yes," she said as his arm tightened around her shoulders. "It's been that." What a pleasure it was to stand so close to a man as obviously blessed as Gregory Stewart. His big, strong body radiated health and a virile pleasure in life and all things physical. How avidly she'd watched him today, drinking in the sight of his muscular back as he swam laps in the pool. Simple things like the sparkle of the sun on his dark hair; his irreverent sense of humor; the tenderness he showed to the girls and to Joey—why, she'd felt fourteen again and madly infatuated with the quarterback on the Newtown High School football team.

He turned her toward him, enveloping her in his embrace—and she *was* fourteen again, foolish and awkward and painfully aware of each breath she took, each beat of her wild, young heart.

"It's getting late," she managed at last, just as the deep silence threatened to turn meaningful. "I need to bathe the girls and get them ready for bed."

He stroked her hair with the palm of his hand in long, languorous movements that caressed her scalp and made her entire body tingle with pleasure.

"You're throwing me out," he said in a voice as dark and vibrant as the star-filled sky.

"It's only fair. You did the same to Mary Ann and Joey."

"Play by the rules, do you, Diana?"

"Yes," she said, meeting his gaze. "I'm afraid I do." She

knew all about the rules between men and women, and where she and Gregory Stewart were headed was someplace she wasn't ready to go—at least, not yet.

"I want to see you again."

"Dave invited me to see the baby the day after tomorrow."

"I can't wait that long."

Her laugh was high and extremely pleased. "I have to start working, Gregory, and you have an animal hospital to run."

"Lunch tomorrow."

"I'm sorry. No."

"Dinner."

"Gregory, I—"

He kissed her hard on the mouth. "Breakfast?"

It was scandalous, the way her hips seemed to melt into his. "I'm a relentless schedule-maker, remember? Tomorrow is strictly work."

"I can't tempt you?"

"Oh, yes, you can tempt me, but I won't relent." She kissed the cleft in his chin. "We can go to the hospital together to see Peggy, if you'd like."

"There are a few things I'd like better."

Her body swayed toward him, and she placed her palms against his chest to keep from totally disgracing herself.

"I'll take you to dinner afterwards."

"That would be wonderful, Gregory, but I'm a package deal these days."

"We'll find a place with high chairs. I want to get to know you better."

She forced air into her burning lungs and reason into her brain. "I'm only here for the month," she said lightly. "You'll have to settle for what you can learn in the next twenty-seven days."

"And I'm leaving August 15," he answered, cupping her face between his massive hands. "We'll have to move fast."

"I—mmm—the girls and I are a package deal, Gregory."

He pressed a kiss into the hollow at the base of her throat. "You said that before."

"I don't think you understand. I take the responsibility seriously. I don't want them to see or hear anything they might not understand." *I don't want to make any mistakes. The next time I fall for a man, I want to be sure he's the right one.*

He watched her carefully. "I know what you're saying, Diana."

"I'm not sure that you do. I—there really isn't an easy way to say this. I'm not looking for summer romance, Gregory, for something temporary." She breathed deeply and took the plunge. "Oh, damn! What I'm saying is, I don't sleep around."

He didn't laugh, and her feelings took another sharp and dangerous turn as he met her eyes. "I'd like to spend time with you while you're here."

"No strings?"

"No strings."

"Well," she said slowly, "I'd like that."

"Good," said Gregory, lowering his mouth to hers.

"Good," said Diana, moving into his kiss.

"Fat chance," said Boris.

Chapter Eleven

"Something's wrong," said Paula the next morning. "I can hear it in your voice."

"You can't hear anything in my voice." Diana yawned as she switched the receiver from her left ear to her right. "You haven't given me the chance to say anything."

"It's in what you're *not* saying," her sister persisted.

"It's six o'clock in the morning here, Paulie, and I had to run a mile and a half to answer this blasted phone. If you're looking for brilliant conversation, call someone else."

"Where are the girls?"

"Asleep, just like I was before you called."

"Where are they sleeping?"

"I told you: I have junior beds in the master bedroom with me."

"And you're downstairs?" Paula cried. "What if they try to climb onto that monstrosity of a bed?"

"Don't worry," Diana said, stifling another yawn. "I thought of everything. Fort Knox isn't as safe as they are."

"Just because you write that column doesn't mean you know everything, Diana. Wait until you become a mother. You'll—"

"—know just how hard it is. I've heard it before, Paula." She didn't bother to stifle her third yawn. "Is there anything else, or can I get a little sleep before your next phone call?"

"Excuse me for worrying about my own children!" Paula snapped.

"I'm sorry," said Diana, "but you're beginning to make me feel as if you don't trust me."

"Of course I trust you."

"Then why all the questions?"

There was a long silence, then the muffled sound of crying at the other end of the line.

"Paula?"

"I miss them, that's why!"

Diana's heart softened. "They're okay, Paulie, I promise you. In fact, they had such a grand time at our barbecue yesterday that they'll probably sleep in." Which meant until all of seven-thirty or eight.

Paula sniffled audibly. "Did the veterinarian show up?"

"Yes, he did."

"And—"

"And nothing. He brought his receptionist and her son and his partner and his pregnant wife."

"Pregnant? How far along?"

"Would you believe she went into labor during supper?"

"Did you make that potato salad you always make?"

"Of course."

"No wonder," said Paula with a laugh. "That stuff is lethal."

Oh great, thought Diana. Not only wasn't she moving forward on compiling material for her book; now she was moving backward. "Everyone else seemed to like it."

"How about the good doctor?"

"He ate enough of it."

"That's not what I'm talking about. How about the good doctor and you?"

Voluptuous ripples of sensation rose from the soles of her feet as she remembered the kisses shared in that very kitchen. "I enjoy his company," she said carefully. "We'll be going to see Dave and Peggy's baby tomorrow."

"Beware of summer romances," her sister intoned. "They can break your heart."

"You sound like Boris," Diana said. "Have no fear, Paulie. Neither one of us is interested in broken hearts."

"A word of caution seemed apropos."

"I appreciate it, but I seriously doubt my heart is in any significant danger." She reached into the refrigerator and withdrew a carton of orange juice. "Besides, I'll only be here another twenty-six days." *And he'll be gone by mid-August.*

"I know this may be hard for you to believe, but not everything in life follows a timetable." Her sister's voice grew distant and dreamy. "Art and I only knew each other eight days before we got married."

"Don't say things like that. The whole idea makes me extremely nervous. It's a miracle you two are still together."

"The miracle is that I found him, Di. Staying together's the easy part, when it's right."

"From your mouth to God's ear," Diana muttered. If Mary Ann Marino thought Diana was an optimist, she would find Paula downright loony. How she'd love to be the one to introduce those two polar opposites.

"Keep your eyes open," Paula commanded in her best married-sister tone of voice. "You never know when the right man will come around the corner."

"Well, he'd better not come until I've lost weight," Diana said, pouring orange juice into a Big Bird paper cup.

"Maybe it's too late. Maybe you've already met him."

"Maybe you've lost your mind."

"I have a sixth sense about such things, Di, and I have a feeling—"

"Sleep well, Paula, and good night."

An answering machine, she thought.

Definitely.

THE WOMAN'S EYES were anxious and bright with tears. "How is he?"

"It was touch and go, but I think he'll make it."

"Will there be any side effects?"

"Some slight swelling, but nothing serious. Compresses should do the trick."

The elderly woman's smile was a sight to behold as she clasped Gregory to her pouter-pigeon bosom. "You know how dear Jo-Jo is to me, Doctor. Words seem insufficient to express my thanks."

He kissed her cheek and extricated himself from her Chanel No. 5 embrace. "You'll have Jo-Jo with you quite a few more years, Mrs. Burton."

"When can he come home, Doctor?"

"How does tomorrow morning sound?"

"I shall be here when your doors open!"

He walked Mrs. Burton to the front door, then locked it behind her and closed the blinds. How little it took in the scheme of things to make a person happy. Keeping an old woman and her ancient terrier together a bit longer wasn't front-page material, but it probably did more for Mrs. Burton's health and well-being than the latest wonder drug.

And it did a hell of a lot more for him than all the fancy parties and seminars he'd hosted back in the old days, when he'd served as the glamour boy darling of the New York Animal Hospital in Manhattan, catering to the pampered pets of the equally pampered carriage trade.

He'd arrived in New York fresh from veterinary school, filled with lofty ideas about the relationship between man and beast and how noble it was to care for the lowest of God's creatures.

Before he knew what hit him, he found himself guesting on all the talk shows, lending his name to a book for Doubleday, putting together a video on pet care—"Smile, Gregory darling, smile!"—and, not incidentally, falling in love with media-savvy socialite Hayley Carter Caldwell. He'd led a charmed life and had had no reason to believe things would change—until three weeks after his thirtieth birthday, when he was diagnosed as having Hodgkin's disease, and he stopped being a golden boy and started being a man.

A man who was sick. A man who was scared. A man who had needed a hand to hold in the darkest hours of the night, when he wanted to give up the ghost and end the pain.

There was nothing like a bout with cancer to show you who your true friends were—and Gregory discovered in record time that the word ''cancer'' was the most powerful four-letter word of them all. Friends fell away from him like autumn leaves from a windblown oak tree. He grew skinny and bald and short-tempered; the reporters and photographers and society groupies looked for greener pastures.

And he found that it didn't matter. He discovered he was stronger than he'd imagined, more self-sufficient, more determined—and if that determination sometimes looked like selfishness, so be it. He walked through the fire for two long years and came out the other side.

Alone.

He quit the New York Animal Hospital, sold his co-op on Central Park West and juggled his priorities. He also discovered that Hayley loved the spotlight more than she loved him, and not even that was enough to shake his conviction. He knew what he wanted and how to get it; he understood in a way few people did that time was precious, and determined never to waste time doing anything he didn't want to do.

He left Manhattan behind and never looked back. He made new friends, established a thriving veterinary practice and gained stature in the community. Although he did volunteer work for a local Cancer Care affiliate, he'd been able to divorce himself from the disease that had almost taken his life until the day Joey Marino was diagnosed. Then it all came rushing back at him—the cold sweats, the fiery nightmares, the dark fear that he'd gotten off too easily, that he didn't deserve what he had, that somehow, sometime he would have to pay for his good fortune—even though he had already paid dearly for the privilege of life.

He wished he could give his strength to Joey, but that was a fool's errand. There was nothing he could do for the boy, nothing Mary Ann could do. It was all written down somewhere, and nothing anybody could say or do would change it. Certainly his staying in East Hampton wouldn't change things, no matter what Mary Ann said. Damn it, he loved the kid, but this trip was his prize for staying the course, and he intended to be out on the high seas when he hit the magic, five-year mark and was officially deemed "cured." He'd earned these three months sailing the Caribbean, and if at times his conscience nudged at him—well, he'd discovered years ago that the road Joey was on was a road you could only walk by yourself.

Better the kid learn it now.

He turned and strode back into his private office and looked down at Daisy and her pups, asleep on their bed of newspaper and straw. What was wrong with him, anyway? All he did was give Mrs. Burton some good news, and suddenly he was thinking about things he'd believed buried deep in his subconscious.

Maybe it was the weather.

"Get real, Stewart," he mumbled, reduced to talking to himself.

It was Diana Travis. Ditzy, foolish, opinionated, *lovely* Diana Travis with the two little nieces and the fat cat—and the oddest way of making him feel more alive than he had in years.

He'd see her again tomorrow. He'd see the dimples in her cheeks as she smiled, hear the sweet, clear sound of her laughter, feel her skin so soft and tender beneath his hands tomorrow. He'd—

Tomorrow?

He'd see her tonight, or know the reason why.

THE MOST AMAZING THING about the fifth of July was the fact that Diana actually unpacked her computer and got it set up on the rented stand at the far end of the solarium. While she hadn't done any real work, save for shuffling and re-shuffling the ream of notes she'd accumulated, at least she was ready to begin.

The second most amazing thing was the fact that she had somehow managed to keep herself from picking up the telephone and calling Gregory.

He had been on her mind constantly, from the moment his car disappeared down the driveway last night until right this very moment. He had even featured prominently in a number of dreams that were quite explicit—and quite delightful. Why had she ever been foolish enough to believe that not seeing him today would make her more inclined to settle down and work?

"Because you're an idiot," she said out loud as she sat down on a plastic lawn chair in front of the television set. Obviously she wasn't going to do anything more challenging than eat dinner, play with the girls, and consider—however briefly—the possibility of doing some serious work. What on earth had happened to the organized, efficient, *disciplined* Diana Travis of just a few days ago? It seemed that from the moment she climbed into the rented station wagon and headed toward East Hampton, Diana's entire life had taken a one-hundred-eighty-degree turn into something that resembled a 1930s screwball comedy.

Would the *real* Diana have been sitting there, eating leftover potato salad and laughing as Laverne and Shirley argued about who was the best bottle-capper in Milwaukee? Would the *real* Diana have let five, perfectly fine workdays slip away, while she played with the twins and swam in the pool and wasted ten dollars in quarters on that ridiculous bathroom slot machine?

Unfortunately the *real* Diana was nowhere in sight, and the current Diana Travis was more than willing to spend her time eating, sleeping and daydreaming about the gorgeous Dr. Stewart.

She fed the girls during *Happy Days*, and was back in front of the tube by the time the theme song for *The Mary Tyler Moore Show* was almost over. Who said she'd lost her scheduling talent, anyway?

Their stomachs filled, the twins were playing on the floor

of the solarium, while Boris watched over them with a mournful eye. "Read the instructions!" the bird cackled as the girls labored to build a castle with their red, white and blue blocks. Ignatius, sprawled atop the television set like a decadent prince, merely yawned. Mary Richards was screwing up her courage to ask Mr. Grant for a raise, when the front doorbell rang. Diana nearly dropped her glass of iced tea in surprise.

The repo man? she wondered as she headed through the endless foyer. A short man in a bad suit had made a surprise visit to Gull Cottage that morning, not long after Paula's phone call, to retrieve the antique wall clock and the papier-mâché shark. What could be next?

She straightened the hem on her shorts and smoothed her T-shirt, then opened the door wide.

"I'm through with waiting!" Gregory Stewart, large and male and extremely determined, swung her up into his muscular arms and carried her into the foyer, kicking the heavy door closed behind him. "We're running out of time."

With that, he covered her mouth with his, in a kiss that was even more demanding than those they had shared less than twenty-four hours before.

"Gregory, what on earth—?"

"Quiet," he said, then kissed her again.

"What on earth has gotten into you?" she managed after she caught her breath.

"We only have twenty-six days left. I'll be damned if I waste them."

Her heart throbbed painfully inside her chest. This shouldn't be happening...her schedule...her weight...and it wasn't anywhere near Labor Day yet....

But there she was in the arms of the most splendid man she'd ever seen, dizzied by his kisses, swept away on a wave of sheer emotion unlike anything she'd ever experienced before.

"Are you going to call the police on me?" Gregory demanded.

She blinked, trying to clear away the haze of passion that clouded her vision. "Are you dangerous?"

"Yes." His breath was hot and sweet against her skin. "Very."

"Good," she said, delighting in the sensation of being cradled in his powerful arms. "I like dangerous men."

He kissed her jaw, her throat, his teeth nipping sharply at the sensitive flesh in a way that made her gasp with pleasure. "God, you smell wonderful," he murmured, his mouth pressed against her ear as she melted against his chest.

"Are you sweeping me off my feet, Dr. Stewart?"

"Any objections?"

"I'll let you know."

"We have no time to waste."

"You're right," she said dreamily, wrapping her arms tightly about his neck. "Kiss me again."

"My pleasure."

Oh, no, she thought as his mouth claimed hers. *That's where you're wrong, Dr. Stewart.* The pleasure was most definitely hers. She felt tiny in his arms, delicate and cherished and more womanly than she'd felt in a very long time. His chest was a solid wall of muscle, warm and hard and wonderfully male; he smelled of sunshine and sea air and the subtle, indefinable scent of desire.

He drew his tongue along the place where her lips met, coaxing, tempting, and she needed no encouragement to allow him entry to her mouth, gasping at the force and heat of his possession. His tongue slid deeper into the moist cavern, thrusting, the rhythm quickening until it matched the furious thundering of her blood.

From somewhere came the sound of laughter, high and girlish, but Diana pushed it from her consciousness. There wasn't room for anything save the sound and scent and sight of him—and the staircase that beckoned them upstairs. She'd cut her teeth on *Gone with the Wind* and knew full well the significance of a sweeping staircase—and of a man strong enough to whisk the woman he wanted into his arms and carry her upstairs without his legs buckling beneath him.

His grip on her tightened; she could almost imagine she felt his muscles swelling with renewed power. This was a man who could give Rhett Butler a run for his money.

This was...

"We have company."

This voice she couldn't dismiss as her imagination—not with his lips against the curve of her throat the way they were. Her eyes fluttered open, as if she was awakening from a deep sleep.

"Wh-what?"

He inclined his head toward the ground. "Take a look."

Kath and Jenny were entwined around Gregory's knees and looking up at them in open curiosity.

"Me! Me!" they cried in unison. "Up!"

"I don't believe it," Diana said into Gregory's shoulder.

"I do," he said. "They have their mother's sense of timing."

How could she have forgotten her curly-haired chaperones? "I think you'd better put me down."

Carefully, he set Diana down. "I thought they'd be asleep by now"

"Not for another hour."

"Makes you wish it wasn't daylight saving time, doesn't it?"

The truth was, it made Diana wish quite a number of things, most of which she couldn't tell him in front of the twins.

Kath and Jenny tugged again at his pants leg and raised their volume. "Up!"

"I think they mean business," Diana said.

With a good-natured shrug he scooped them up into his arms, and Diana fought with a ridiculous surge of envy directed toward her very own nieces.

"Have you had dinner?" he asked.

"Potato salad."

He made a face. "There's a good Chinese place in town. Best shredded beef for miles."

"Afraid not." She gestured toward the two little girls in his arms. "It's almost their bedtime."

"We could find a sitter."

"I don't think so, Gregory."

"Looks like we have a problem, doesn't it?"

Her heart sank at the look on his handsome face. "I guess it does."

"We could have had a terrific dinner. Hot-and-sour soup, dim sum, broccoli in garlic sauce—"

"I really wish you wouldn't do this, Gregory. You're not making this very easy." She had willingly taken on the responsibility of caring for the girls but, truth to tell, she'd never expected someone like Gregory Stewart to come along and disrupt her carefully scheduled month at Gull Cottage. "If you feel like going out for Chinese, by all means, go out for Chinese."

"You mean that?"

She nodded. "With all my heart." *Don't go. I'll feed you potato salad and leftover fried chicken and all the cheesecake you can eat. Please stay....*

"Well, if you're sure—" He handed the twins to her, and before she could say another word, he left.

"Bye-bye!" Jenny and Kath waved at the closed front door while Diana stood in the center of the foyer, shell-shocked.

"You stinker," she said, as the girls looked up at her. "You absolute stinker."

"Man bad?" asked Jenny, eyes wide.

Before Diana had a chance to answer, the doorbell chimed. It couldn't be.

She swung the door open again.

It was.

Gregory Stewart stood there on the step, arms laden with fragrant parcels. "Szechuan Palace, at your service."

"You had it in your car all the time?"

He nodded. "I knew you couldn't leave the kids."

"And you were baiting me?"

"Not baiting you. I was heightening the suspense."

"I'll give you suspense!" She slammed the door in his face.

"Man bad," said Kath to her sister.

"That's right," said Diana. "Man *very* bad. Man rotten. Man terrible."

The doorbell rang for the third time.

Man persistent.

"Go away," she called out. "We don't want any."

He opened the door himself. "Where should I put it?"

"You don't really want me to answer that, do you?"

"We're going to have to work on your sense of humor, Diana."

"My sense of humor doesn't need any work."

"You need to loosen up."

"I don't want to loosen up," she said through clenched teeth.

He followed her into the kitchen and deposited his packages on the countertop. "If you want me to leave, just say the word and I'm out of here."

Last chance, Travis. Send him away now, or you're a goner.

"Diana?" The sparkle was gone from his eyes, and in its place was something deeper, something stronger, something infinitely more tempting than simple desire.

"Stay," she said at last, giving herself up to the inevitable. "I want you to stay."

Chapter Twelve

Gregory helped her with the girls, bathing and changing and tucking them in with the ease of a man comfortable with the tender side of his nature. Diana found herself casting quick glances at him as he crouched between the girls' beds and told them a rollicking story about Daisy the cocker spaniel and Ignatius the cat and their adventures on the high seas.

She was behind schedule on meeting her book deadline for Mother's column, but was it possible—was there any chance at all that she was ahead of schedule on finding the man of her dreams?

Dangerous thoughts, those, and she pushed them from her mind as they carried their Chinese feast out to the deck.

"I don't think I've ever had a Szechuan picnic before," she said as they set up the paper carton on the twins' plastic table. "Is this an old East Hampton tradition?"

"If it isn't, it should be." He opened the lid on the container of hot-and-sour soup and handed her a plastic spoon. "Dive in."

They ate dinner in a companionable silence, watching as darkness spread over the Atlantic. Now and again a rocket, left over from the Fourth, exploded over the beach, casting gold and silver glitter across the night sky, battling the stars above for dominance.

"I could get used to this," Diana said as a cool breeze

blew in off the ocean. "I never knew I could be so downright lazy."

"This is your vacation, isn't it?"

She drained her bottle of beer and leaned against Gregory's shoulder. "Working vacation," she amended. "Or at least that's what I told my agent and editor."

"I thought you were starting work today."

"I was. You interrupted."

His laugh rumbled pleasantly against her ear. "I interrupted *The Mary Tyler Moore Show*."

"I was going to start work right after it."

"A likely story. I saw the *TV Guide* next to your chair. You had four more shows circled in red pencil."

"Handy household hint #376: plan your children's TV time carefully."

"Those weren't kid shows you had circled."

"Okay, so that's handy household hint #377."

He ruffled her curls, those long fingers of his cupping her head. "So you really are the organized type."

"Long ago and far away—I wish you'd known the old me. I used to be efficient and capable and disciplined, down to the last microsecond." She sighed and gestured toward her shorts-clad body. "Look at me now: indolent, lazy and sloppy. If I weren't so comfortable, I'd be ashamed of myself."

"I like you this way."

"The old me was so much better, Gregory. Now I have no willpower whatsoever." She cast a baleful look at the remnants of their Chinese dinner. "And I'm supposed to be on a diet...."

He kissed her temple. "Go back to the part about no willpower."

"Don't rush things, Gregory." His lips against her skin were soft as the summer air. "Let's take it slow."

"You'll be gone in twenty-six days, Diana. I don't—"

She pressed the tip of an index finger to his mouth. "I leave Gull Cottage the end of the month, but I'm not leaving the country." She was free and unfettered and able to hang her hat anywhere she chose.

"I am."

She started in surprise. "I'd forgotten." Her lighthearted mood took a sudden shift toward melancholy. There really was no point to all this, was there? She angled her head to look at him. "Tahiti complex?"

"Not really. It's been in the works for a long time." She listened as he told her about the work he intended to do, monitoring the progress of humpback whales for Greenpeace, but she had the distinct feeling there was more to the story than he chose to tell.

"What about the hospital?"

"Dave can handle it. Things ease off after Labor Day, and he has Charlie to help out."

"And that volunteer work you do in Southold?"

"They'll survive. They're closed from Labor Day until the first day of spring."

She hesitated a moment. "And Joey?"

"He knows my plans."

"What does he think about them?"

"What's he going to think about them?" he countered. "He wishes he could cut school and sign on as first mate."

She sensed a tension in him that hadn't been there before. "Sounds like a normal twelve-year-old's reaction to me," she said, keeping her voice light. "He idolizes you, Gregory. You should have seen the way he—"

Greg grasped her shoulders, cutting her off, and pulled her into his embrace. "Can we stop talking now?"

She looked at his mouth, the dimple in his chin, the sparkle that was back in his blue eyes. "You won't hear another word from me."

But even as she surrendered herself to his kiss, a small part of her remained separate, wondering what it was Gregory Stewart was running from—and why it made her feel so uneasy.

THOMAS EDWARD REILLY was plump and rosy and impossibly adorable. In fact, so were all of the babies in the hospital nursery—a fact that was causing Diana no small amount of trouble.

"I'd love to scoop them up and take them all home with me," she said to Mary Ann the next afternoon, as the two women peered through the heavy, glass window separating adults from infants. "They're precious."

"Look at that one," said Mary Ann, pointing toward a blue-blanketed bundle in the far corner. "He looks like a Cabbage Patch doll."

Up front, Thomas Reilly screwed up his tiny, red face and squalled lustily. "Peggy's going to have her hands full with that little guy. He has incredible lung power."

"I told her to catch up on her sleeping in the hospital, because it will be eighteen years before she has an unbroken night's rest from this point on."

"Come on, Mary Ann," Diana objected. "The twins sleep through the night, and they're not even two and a half yet."

"Company manners," said Mary Ann. "Wait until the monsters in the closet arrive and the tooth fairy and the fourteen glasses of water and the fourteen trips to the bathroom. And that's only for starters."

"You must tremble at the thought of Joey's first date. Why, I'd—" The expression on Mary Ann's face changed, and Diana wished she could call back her words. "Maybe we should be heading down to the lobby. Gregory and Joey have probably had enough of baby-sitting duty. I'm sure they want to see Dave and Peggy once more before we leave."

Mary Ann said nothing. Her head was bent forward, until her curly red bangs brushed the glass window.

"Newborns do it to me, too," Diana said as a knot of fear, ugly and dark, settled in her belly. "I disgraced myself the day the twins were born, blubbering all over my brother-in-law. You would have thought I'd given birth to them, the way I carried on."

Gregory had been so optimistic when they'd talked about

Joey's condition, so positive the boy was on the road to recovery that Diana had pushed the other possibility from her mind.

And because Diana didn't have anything miraculous in her bag of tricks—no potions or powders or incantations to ward away evil—she simply put her arms around the red-haired woman and wished she could transfer some of her own optimism to Mary Ann.

THE GROUP OF THEM stopped at a Burger King in Riverhead for dinner, and the twins were enchanted by the cardboard crowns the counter clerk presented to them. They insisted upon wearing them throughout dinner, even though the crowns kept slipping off and falling to the floor; Joey took it upon himself to retrieve the paper tiaras and place them back on the girls' heads each time it happened.

Mary Ann smoked a lot and ate very little; her dark-shadowed, blue eyes rarely left her son's face. Joey ate half a Whopper and an order of fries, and dawdled over a chocolate shake while he urged the twins to stop wearing their food and start eating it.

Gregory seemed oblivious of the undercurrent of tension at the table. He ate with gusto, laughing and talking as if everything was normal. Men so often seemed unaware of the fluctuations in the emotional barometer, and the heretofore perfect Dr. Stewart was apparently no exception. In a way Diana was glad to find his Achilles' heel.

The twins giggled over their milk-shake mustaches, while Diana and Joey held a lively debate on pet care. The boy was a marvel. He seemed to know everything there was to know about dogs and cats and birds.

"Boy, could I use you around Gull Cottage," she said, laughing. "Need a part-time job?"

"Do you mean it?" Joey asked.

"Sure," said Diana, glancing at his mother. "That is, if Mary Ann says okay."

"Please, Ma!"

Mary Ann looked at her son for a long moment, then shrugged her narrow shoulders. "Oh, why not? I always wanted to be a two-paycheck family."

Joey let out a whoop of excitement that Diana was sure they heard all the way back to East Hampton.

Finally the meal was over, and they stood out in the parking lot as traffic whizzed by on Route 25A.

"You don't have to start tomorrow," Diana said to Joey, as Gregory and Mary Ann fastened the twins into their car seats. "If you want to begin next week, that's okay with me."

"I'm saving for a catcher's mitt," Joey said, straightening the bill of his Yankee baseball cap. "I want to work as many days as I can. It's not easy to find a job around here."

"No," said Diana, grinning at the boy's enthusiasm, "I guess it's not." Twelve-year-olds weren't in great demand in the job market. "How does around nine o'clock sound?"

"How about eight-thirty?" Mary Ann chimed in. "Then I can still get to work on time myself."

"I'm all in favor of that," said Gregory with a laugh. "We have a lot to get straightened out before I take off for the Caribbean."

"I'm outnumbered," Diana said with a good-natured shrug. "Eight-thirty it is." She waggled a finger in Joey's direction. "Just don't expect me to be an intelligent boss until I've had my second cup of coffee."

"Can I clean Boris's cage?"

"Good grief," Diana turned to Mary Ann. "Is this boy for real?"

"Afraid so. He loves animals almost as much as he loves the Yankees."

"Cleaning Boris's cage isn't part of the job description, Joey, but you're welcome to it." She named a dollar figure that was twenty-five cents higher than the original hourly wage. "Okay?"

"Aw-right!" Joey's narrow face was lighted from within

by excitement. "I bet I'll have enough for the catcher's mitt before the summer's over."

"Yeah," said Gregory, his voice huskier than usual. "I'll bet you will, at that."

THE TEST RESULTS were bad, Gregory...test results were bad...bad...bad....

Mary Ann's words haunted him as he drove Diana and the girls back to Gull Cottage in her rented station wagon. He thought he'd done a fair job of keeping his emotions under control, but back at Burger King he'd come close to losing it. He was glad Diana and the twins were dozing, because it gave him a chance to untangle the knot his gut was in.

A mistake. It had to be a mistake. The kid was doing better every day. He could see it—would Joey actually be asking to clean Boris's cage, if he was feeling as lousy as those doctors apparently wanted him to believe? The kid had fire and energy and too much spirit to give in to a couple of misread blood tests.

What the hell was the matter with everyone, anyway—jumping to conclusions like that? Best thing for Joey was to go on doing what he wanted to do: working for Diana; saving for his catcher's mitt; taking each day as it came. Last thing the kid needed was a bunch of doom-saying crepe hangers.

Jackasses, he thought, slowing down to avoid a cat scampering across the dark road. The kid was fine, just fine. Joey would breeze through his treatments this summer, and come September he'd be back in school, where he should be, while Gregory would be out on the open seas, according to plan.

Dave would be back at work in two weeks—maybe he could even aim toward the end of July. The season had been slow so far, and with Charlie on staff now, the work load was easier to handle. A vision of Joey's sad eyes flashed before him, and he forced the image away.

You've earned the right, he told himself. Finally he had the time and the money to take off, to push aside all of his responsibilities and run, the way he'd wanted to run from the first day he'd been told he had cancer. And he wasn't running away from anything—Joey and Mary Ann weren't his family. Joey had a mother and a father and a slew of relatives willing to hold his hand when he needed it.

Nobody had been there to hold Gregory's hand, and he'd survived it. Besides, the kid would be fine. One day Joey Marino would be coming up fast on the official all clear the same as Gregory, and he'd understand.

Next to him Diana stirred, and for a moment he wondered what he would do if she asked him to stay.

"Ridiculous," he mumbled as they entered the village of East Hampton. After August 1, she'd be gone, and he would be only a memory.

Why then did she make him think of things he hadn't thought about in years? About family and permanence and putting down the kind of roots he'd believed existed only in Frank Capra movies and 1950s television.

She was a dazzling mass of contradictions: uncertain about her appeal, charming, so insanely positive the world was a happy place that she drew people toward her as if she were a magnet. She was also arrogant and stubbornly certain that some crazy, fairy godmother was ready to grant all her wishes.

She radiated womanly warmth with her nieces; she was patient and loving with Joey; she offered Mary Ann friendship, even when Mary Ann was being caustic and downright rude. In his arms she was pure female heat. Even Ignatius and Boris were treated to a degree of loving care that Gregory as a boy would have gotten down on his knees and thanked God for.

She expected the best from herself and those around her, and damned if she didn't seem to get it. Her gentle, innately feminine nature was bolstered by a spine of pure steel, and Gregory found himself wondering how it would feel to be loved by a woman like that.

He wanted to hear her voice, see the sunlight dance in her hair, hold her close for as long as he could. He wanted—

He glanced into the rearview mirror and laughed out loud. "What a fool," he mumbled in the silent car.

He wanted August to hurry up and yet wished July would never end.

Lots of luck, Stewart. He might as well try to stop time completely because, like it or not, the end was definitely in sight.

Chapter Thirteen

Joey Marino turned out to be a godsend. He cleaned Boris's cage until it sparkled. He fed and combed Ignatius until the Abyssinian's coat gleamed. He watched *Sesame Street* with Kath and Jenny, then took them down to the beach at low tide to search for sand crabs, while Diana sat at the foot of the dunes with her laptop computer and notebook.

With Joey around to play with the girls and answer some of their endless questions, Diana was able to watch over all three of them and still get down to work. It felt good to be back on familiar territory, dealing with broken dishes and broken hearts. She dispatched advice on everything from the perfect wedding cake to the perfect man with renewed enthusiasm, pulling favorite bits from past columns, quoting suggestions from loyal readers, and surprising herself with inspired bits of philosophy and down-home common sense.

The work went so well that within three days she was back on schedule and then some. She must have been mad to think she could carry off a column like "Mother Knows Best" without firsthand experience; this time spent caring for her nieces had opened her eyes to the awesome responsibilities involved in raising a family. It didn't dampen her enthusiasm for raising a family of her own, but it did cause her respect for women like Mary Ann Marino to soar.

And it certainly made her sister's dithering seem comical. "I don't want to hear it," Diana said one morning near the end of her second week at Gull Cottage. "If you ever complain about caring for the girls again, I'll hit you over the head with a loaf of French bread."

Paula's insulted huff was crystal clear, thanks to AT & T and the wonders of fiber-optic cables. "Don't criticize me until you've walked in my shoes, little sister."

"I have walked in your shoes, Paulie, and I admit it's a tight fit, but what Mary Ann Marino is going through is a whole different ball game. I hope you thank God every night for two healthy children."

"You must be back at work. You sound like last year's Mother's Day column."

"I'm serious, Paulie. You don't know how lucky you are."

"I *do* know how lucky I am," said an aggrieved Paula. "Why do you think I'm driving Art crazy about coming home early?"

Diana's heart did a double thump inside her chest. "Are you serious?"

"Very. I miss them so much, even Monte Carlo can't hold my interest."

"When you say early, just how early do you mean?" *I don't want this to be over yet, Paulie. There's so much I have to do....* The thought of leaving Gregory caused a lump, painful and huge, to form in her throat.

"I'd come home today if I thought Art wouldn't shoot me," her sister said, "but I guess I'll hang on. It's already July 13—just eighteen more days until I see them again."

"Eighteen more days," said Diana as she hung up the telephone and gazed out the kitchen window at the twins and Joey, who were eating breakfast on the deck. Eighteen more days, and she'd be packing up the station wagon once again and leaving all of this behind, as if it had never happened.

As if it had never happened? Who was she trying to kid? In less than two weeks her entire existence had been turned upside down. Her fancy theories on easy parenting had flown out the window. Her pretty notions on single motherhood had gone up in flames. In a life that had been happily scheduled to the last millisecond, Diana found herself forgetting to check her watch and taking time now and again to simply enjoy herself.

Gregory's easygoing approach to life had rubbed off on her. He took his veterinary practice seriously, but made it perfectly clear that he was only in business because he *wanted* to be, not because he had to be. He spent his time doing what he wanted, when he wanted, and his wholehearted embrace of pleasure was hard to resist. Not even Joey's illness, as painfully obvious as it had become, was enough to daunt Gregory's spirits, and her heart swelled with unnamed emotions as she watched the man do his best to pass his strength onto the boy.

It was perfectly obvious that Gregory Stewart was one of life's lucky ones. Blessed by the gods with good fortune and good friends, he was an enviable physical specimen, whose striking looks were only surpassed by an extraordinarily fine spirit.

Diana sighed. Maybe the Fates had known what they were doing, after all, by introducing her to the perfect man at the most imperfect time. What earthly good could there be in becoming involved with a man who was heading for the high seas the first chance he got? She wanted more than a summer fling; the one caper she'd allowed herself since her divorce had been such an unmitigated failure that she'd determined to leave casual romantic encounters for those better suited to them.

Gregory Stewart, however, was quite a temptation. He turned the simple act of kissing into an Olympic event—one in which he was definitely a gold medalist.

Diana knew that different rules applied at different times, and summer resorts were an entity unto themselves. Most men in Gregory's position would be taking full advantage of that fact. Most men would have taken one look at the chaos in Gull Cottage and fled for the nearest singles' bar.

Not Gregory Stewart. He'd seen to Boris's hypochondria,

listened to the girls' endless stories about Cinderella and Miss Piggy, and shown Diana a fierce, yet tender sensuality that could easily be her undoing.

Somehow their disparate lives fitted together as if they were two pieces of a larger puzzle, and she couldn't help but wish she'd be around long enough to see the finished picture.

Foolish thoughts, for even if she stayed on beyond her time at Gull Cottage, come August 15, the admirable Dr. Stewart would set sail for the Caribbean, leaving her alone to embark upon her great husband hunt.

"You shouldn't be doing this," she mumbled as she reached for the East Hampton telephone directory on the countertop.

"Totally insane," she said as she dialed Mrs. Geller's number at the real estate office.

"It's better this way," she declared as she placed the receiver back on its cradle. After all, they'd never even had an official date. Not really. She hadn't primped for him; he hadn't brought her flowers; she hadn't sailed off on a cloud of L'Air du Temps as he swept her away in his black Corvette for a candlelight supper and untold delights.

If Gull Cottage had been available for the month of August, she just might have done something very stupid—something that would have obliterated her bank account, devastated her work schedule, and quite possibly left her with a broken heart.

Unfortunately, she had the sinking feeling it would have been worth it.

THERE WAS no doubt about it, thought Diana next evening. This was definitely a date.

A small, candle-lighted restaurant with a view of the ocean. A table for two, complete with roses and champagne. An elegant meal, served on real china, instead of the paper plates she'd grown used to.

And Gregory.

Who said fantasies never came true?

"More champagne?" he asked.

She held out her glass. "I'd adore it." "Mother Knows Best" might extol the virtues of jelly-jar glasses and hamburger dinners, but Diana was taking indecent pleasure in Moët et Chandon and steak chateaubriand.

After the last two weeks of *Sesame Street* and Mr. Rogers, she'd almost forgotten what it was like to slip into her Laura Ashley sundress and strappy, white sandals, and not have to worry about peanut butter kisses and chocolate-stained hands.

From the moment Mary Ann and Joey showed up on the doorstep two hours ago with two pepperoni pizzas and orders from Gregory to baby-sit the twins, Diana had known it was useless to protest. "Doctor's orders," said Mary Ann, then pushed Diana upstairs to get ready.

How wonderful it felt to brush her hair until the blond curls glistened. How glorious it was to apply perfume to her pulse points and not baby powder. How utterly delightful it was to slip into her silkiest lingerie and pretend Gregory would be there later to help her slip out of it.

And how magnificent he looked, all decked out in a suit and tie, like some almost civilized pirate king.

"Do you like shrimp?" he asked.

"Only if they're large and firm."

He arched a dark brow in her direction, then placed her order without as much as cracking a smile. Dating was more dangerous than she'd imagined it to be; even ordering a simple, seafood cocktail sounded like an invitation to bacchanalia. She'd seen *Tom Jones*. She knew what trouble eating dinner could cause.

As if on cue, the lush, romantic sound of an old Johnny Mathis song filled the room, and couples headed for the dance floor. Diana glanced at Gregory. Dance, that was what they should do. What on earth could happen in the middle of a crowded dance floor?

Two minutes later she had her answer: plenty.

His hands snaked their way up her spine as he drew her close. His hips were pressed against hers in a scandalously thrilling manner that belied the sweet music that surrounded them. Their movements were perfectly matched. Their inner rhythms were wildly synchronous, wildly sensuous, wildly dangerous.

"We used to call this 'make-out music,'" he murmured, his breath hot against the curve of her ear.

"I can see why," she managed.

"It's the rhythm."

"I noticed."

He executed a subtle movement that brought them closer still, a rocking of his hips that was too thrilling to possibly be legal in East Hampton.

"They say you can tell a lot by the way a woman dances."

Diana leaned away so she could look up at him. "You can probably tell I have two left feet."

He told her exactly what else he could tell by the way they fitted together on the dance floor, and she was positive the only thing that kept her from melting right there on the spot was the air-conditioning.

"Maybe we should sit down," she suggested.

"Coward," he said softly as he led her back to their table. "You're only postponing the inevitable."

For once in her life Diana was at a loss for words; for once in her life, Diana was on fire from within.

DURING THE NEXT FEW DAYS Diana learned a great deal about fire and just how easily it could be controlled with two, inquisitive little girls underfoot. She had only to look at Gregory to recreate the wonderful heat she'd experienced that night on the dance floor, and she knew from the kisses they shared on the deck at Gull Cottage that he was finding it as difficult as she to keep the flames under control.

If it weren't for the presence of Kath and Jenny, she had no doubt where they'd end up. Better to keep things light and breezy, Diana reasoned, and she set out to make sightseeing *en famille* her top priority during the rest of her stay at Gull Cottage. Sex was a dangerous game, especially when you knew the man you fancied was heading for the open seas in less than a month.

"You won't *believe* who I saw at the farm stand in Amagansett," Diana said at the beginning of her third week as she, the girls, and Joey burst into the East End Animal Hospital at closing time.

"Lauren Bacall," said Gregory and company in unison.

Diana's jaw sagged. "How did you know?"

Gregory laughed and ruffled her hair. "Sooner or later, everyone out here has a Lauren Bacall story."

"You can make fun of me all you want," said Diana, "but I'm *thrilled.* Lauren Bacall helped me pick tomatoes." She could barely hear herself think over the raucous laughter coming from her so-called friends. "Well, maybe you're used to rubbing elbows with Bogie's baby, but I'm not." Bacall, with that distinctive, contralto voice and the glorious, lined face, had sidled up to Diana at the market and pointed to a basket of absolutely perfect beefsteak tomatoes the greengrocer was putting out. *"Those,"* she had said, with her incomparable timing, "are what I call tomatoes."

Mary Ann draped an arm around her son's shoulders. "So what did you think of Lauren Bacall, kiddo?"

Joey shrugged. "She's old."

Mary Ann made a face. "He thinks anyone over twenty-one is old."

"He didn't think that other fellow was old."

"That was Phil Rizzuto," said Joey, his face animated with excitement at the thought of the Yankees' former shortstop. "That was great!"

Gregory lighted up with excitement himself. "You guys saw the Scooter?"

"Yeah," said Joey, pulling a piece of paper from the pocket of his cutoffs. "I got his autograph, too."

"Now that's something," said Gregory, whistling at the autographed piece of notepaper. "Not everyone has a Phil Rizzuto story."

"I don't believe this!" Diana was outraged. "Here you

have one of the best actresses in the world living right in
your midst, and you get all goofy over some short little man
in dark glasses! Unbelievable.''

"Women," said Gregory, inclining his head toward Diana.
"They don't understand anything, do they, Joey?"

Joey looked at Diana and blushed that adorable shade of
pink she'd grown accustomed to. "She's not so bad," he
mumbled, and Diana was happy that no one laughed.

"JOEY'S GOT IT BAD for you," Gregory observed a half hour
later, as they piled into the station wagon after saying goodbye to the Marinos and to Dave. "Should I be jealous?" He
pulled out of the driveway and headed toward Riverhead and
the north fork, where his boat was docked.

Diana gave him a playful sock in the forearm. "Don't be
silly," she said lightly. "Joey knows my heart belongs to
him." She knew the boy had an adolescent crush on her, and
she was glad that no one had teased him about coming to
her defense in the waiting room.

He was a delightful boy, given to poetic bursts of preteen-
age melodrama that were quickly followed by childish laughter, and tomfoolery that put him on a level with Kath and
Jenny. His admiration for Diana was painfully obvious, and
she found it touching to be the object of his devotion.

Of course, all of this was made the more bittersweet by
the progress of the disease that was ravaging his young body.
Joey was so thin that he barely cast a shadow. Mary Ann's
smoking increased, and it seemed to Diana that the red-haired
woman walked about enshrouded by a thick cloud of cigarette smoke.

She wished she could talk about her fears with Gregory,
but if there was one thing Diana had learned during her stay
in East Hampton, it was to keep those worries to herself.
Gregory was patience unlimited when it came to anything
else, but when the conversation turned to Joey and his illness,
his patience came to a screeching halt. If she said the boy
looked tired, Gregory said he'd never looked better. If she

said the boy looked ill, Gregory changed the subject with the speed of light.

Kath and Jenny were chattering away to each other in the back seat, speaking in an elaborately constructed language that seemed to be three-quarters English and one-quarter their own design.

"Do you understand them?" Gregory asked, cocking his head toward the twins.

"Only after a lot of trial and error. As far as I can tell, they're talking about your boat."

"I hope they're not expecting Trump's yacht. This is a plain, garden variety forty-six-footer."

"There's nothing plain about a forty-six-foot boat, Gregory."

"You're not going to find a solarium and hot and cold running servants."

"Who needs servants? They'd only get in our way."

He grinned at her. "I thought we'd take her out a little way and have dinner on the high seas."

Diana groaned. "What if I get seasick?"

"Do you get seasick?"

"I don't know. I've never been out on the high seas before."

"What about the munchkins?"

"They're old salts. Paula and Art keep a boat at the Jersey shore." She sat up straight in her seat. "Life preservers! Do you have any for the girls?"

"We'll have them fitted at the marina."

His profile was lean and rugged, and her heart did a funny little flip inside her chest. "Thought of everything, did you, Dr. Stewart?"

He glanced toward her, his eyes blue as the sky overhead. "We aim to please."

I'll bet you do, she thought. *Well, here's something else to think about. What would you say if I told you I just might be falling in love?*

GREGORY'S BOAT turned out to be a marvel of fiberglass and
burled wood and brass fittings—over forty feet of perfect
craftsmanship that was a splendid foil for the man who
owned it. The moment they boarded her and he started the
engine, he seemed to grow younger, more carefree, right before her eyes. The day's fatigue slipped away as they left the
marina behind; the slight worry lines on his forehead
smoothed over. With the late-afternoon sun glinting off his
dark hair and his eyes narrowed against the glare, he was the
pirate of her teenage fantasies, come to whisk her away to
some tropical paradise where he would have his way with
her.

She glanced over at the two little girls in their matching
life vests. Ah, well. Her fantasy hadn't included taking the
Bobbsey Twins along for the ride, but this spur-of-the-
moment getaway was wonderful, just the same.

"Look over there," he said, pointing into the distance.
"That's the Connecticut coastline across the Sound. If we'd
gotten an earlier start, we could have had dinner in Mystic."

"Another time," she said, wishing there could be a thousand other times. "We can always bring in a pizza when we
get back to Gull Cottage, or sample the recipes I was working
on for the book."

"Pizza!" Kath piped up as Jenny nodded in agreement.

"Pizza's great," said Gregory, cutting the engine, "but I
had something else in mind."

Diana's eyebrows lifted. "Careful, Doctor," she murmured. "There are minors on board."

"I was talking about dinner."

"We're going back to the marina so soon?"

"I thought we'd dine alfresco."

"Sandwiches?" she asked, wondering where the galley
was. "Fruit and cheese?"

He disappeared below, then a moment later reappeared on
deck with a huge tray, laden with exotic goodies. "Courtesy
of the Hellenic Snack Bar," he said with a flourish. "Only
the best Greek food this side of Athens." He pointed toward

two small plates of plain chicken, rice and broccoli. "I even had something made for the munchkins." She watched, speechless, as he placed the tray on the bolted-down table and whisked out some heavy-duty, paper plates. "It seemed to me it was time to get you out of the kitchen."

Spanakopita.

Moussaka.

Homemade baklava, thick with nuts and honey.

A man who had thought enough of her to not only listen to her likes and dislikes but to *remember* them. A man resourceful enough to understand that the way to a dieting woman's heart was invariably through her stomach.

He was amazing, Gregory Stewart was—amazing and dangerous. Whoever the man of her post-Labor Day dreams turned out to be, he had one heck of a tough act to follow.

HAVING DIANA'S NIECES on board was a little unnerving, Gregory thought, but so far they'd contented themselves with eating their chicken and rice and waving at every fishing boat that passed by. His nightmare of seeing them leap overboard in an attempt to swim to Connecticut hadn't come to pass, but he doubted he'd breathe normally again until they were docked back at the marina.

A breeze blew up off the Sound and ruffled Diana's blond curls. Her lips curved in a gentle smile as she leaned back against the railing and closed her eyes.

Maybe he wouldn't breathe normally again at all. Her white miniskirt rode up her thighs, exposing a long, beautiful length of tanned leg. She wore a cropped, red shirt that barely met the waistband of her skirt, and the swell of her full breasts was outlined by the soft, terry fabric. Her feet were bare, the toenails painted a delicate, shimmering shade of pink. It didn't take a quantum leap of imagination to know how she would feel, naked and willing, in his arms.

"If the girls weren't here, you'd be in a lot of trouble," he said, his voice low and lazy.

"Lucky me." She opened her eyes and gave him a look

through half-closed lids that had him struggling for self-control.

Her breasts were pushing against the terry, and the taut outlines of her nipples were plainly—tantalizingly—visible. He ached to feel their hardness against the palms of his hands.

He cleared his throat; self-control was quickly becoming an exercise in absurdity. "What would you say about taking a trip with me?"

She was silent, watching him through those sleepy, hazel eyes of hers.

Diana had done the impossible—forced him out of his isolation and thrown him headlong back into the mainstream of life. Not only was he spending a great deal of time fantasizing about her, but suddenly he found himself thinking about things he'd given up on a long time ago. About a marriage that would be as much friendship as it was love. About a family of his own, although that was admittedly a long shot. About tossing her over his shoulder and hijacking her to the Caribbean, where they could discover if this was the real thing—or just a glorious facsimile.

In short, the only thing that could make him feel whole and happy and hopeful for the future was knowing that Diana was there at the center of it.

He moved toward her. He couldn't have stopped if he'd wanted to. Every muscle, every fibre in his body was straining toward the inevitable. "I mean it, Diana. What would you say to—?"

"*Ah-choo!*"

Chapter Fourteen

Diana jumped, as if splashed with icy water; Gregory stopped a few feet away from her and looked around. "What was that?"

"A sneeze, I think."

"Yours?"

"No. I thought it was yours."

He shook his head. "Not mine." He started toward her again. "Maybe there's a ghost on board."

"Ah-choo!"

Another sneeze exploded, and Diana reluctantly relinquished passion and went on red alert. "Oh, no!" She wheeled around, just in time to see Kath wipe her nose with her sleeve.

"Are they allergic to something?" Gregory asked.

"Not that I know of." Jenny added her sneeze to that of her sister, and Diana's heart sank. "I can't believe this," she said, then pressed her lips to each small forehead. "They're burning up!" She turned to Gregory. "We have to—"

"Don't worry," he said, "I have it all under control."

As it turned out, Gregory Stewart was a man of his word. Before Diana had a chance to panic, he had them back at the marina and safely bundled into the station wagon. He made a call to Dave, whose brother was married to a pediatrician, and within two and a half hours the girls had been diagnosed, medicated, and tucked into bed for the night.

Diana poured cups of coffee for Gregory and herself, and they strolled onto the deck at Gull Cottage. "Not exactly what you had in mind, was it?"

"Not exactly." Gregory leaned against the railing and took a sip of coffee. "I have to admit those two really had me shook up there. I'm glad they're okay."

"You?" Diana's laugh was high and flavored with the sound of pure, unadulterated relief. "I'm surprised my hair didn't turn white by the time we got to the pediatrician's office."

He reached over and took one of her curls between his large, tanned fingers; her stomach fluttered in a most disconcerting fashion. "How did your sister take the news?"

"The way she takes all news about the kids: I felt like FDR announcing the bombing of Pearl Harbor."

"You told her it was just a summer cold, didn't you?"

"Three times," said Diana with a sigh. "I finally had to give her Dr. Marshall's phone number."

"Dr. Marshall may consider getting a new number."

Diana shot him a quelling look. "Maybe Dr. Marshall can convince Paula to stay in Monte Carlo, where she belongs. Art wasn't having much luck."

Gregory met her eyes. "They might come home?"

"I don't know." She hesitated. The touch of his fingers as they brushed against her neck was heavenly. "Maybe."

He rested his coffee cup on the deck railing and drew closer. "Would they stay here with you?"

"Who knows?" Her breath caught as he looped his other arm around her waist and pulled her toward him. "They might collect the girls and take them back to New Jersey."

"Let's hear it for New Jersey."

She grinned despite herself. "Of course, Art is paying the bills here at Gull Cottage. They'd be within their rights if they stayed a while to enjoy the place."

"There's no furniture inside," Gregory pointed out, then

placed a kiss against the side of her throat. "What would Art think about that?"

A rush of desire, curiously mingled with an odd feeling of contentment, flooded Diana. "Art is a man who loves his creature comforts. I don't think he'd care for it."

"You realize, if the twins weren't on the premises, I wouldn't be so easy to send away, don't you?"

The flutter in her belly intensified. "I had suspected as much."

"Should I call your sister and tell her to come and get her daughters?"

"Gregory, I—" The words stuck in her throat. *Don't ask me, because I don't know if I have the willpower to refuse you anymore.*

His hands slid up over the curve of her waist, along her rib cage, then settled provocatively under the fullness of her breasts.

"No," Diana finally whispered against a rising tide of longing. "Not yet."

He covered her mouth with his, in a kiss that was as demanding as it was tender. "I won't wait forever," he said when he pulled away from her. "Even if it means tossing you over my back and kidnapping you to the high seas."

"Is that a warning?" she asked, trying to keep her voice light.

"It's a promise." He kissed her again, branding her mouth with the shape and taste and texture of his own. "When the month is over, I'm going to claim you."

JOEY LOOKED UP at Diana the next morning, his dark brown eyes wide with disappointment. "If they're sick, that means I've gotta go home, right?"

Diana laughed and waved goodbye to Mary Ann, as the other woman maneuvered her Hyundai back down the curving driveway. "Oh, you're not going to get out of work that easily, Joseph," she said, closing the front door and leading him into the kitchen. "The girls may be under the weather, but that doesn't mean I don't have a lot of chores for you to do today." She narrowed her eyes and looked at him, willing herself to not notice the frightening changes that seemed to be taking place on a daily basis. "That is, if you're in the mood?"

"Sure," said Joey, sitting down at the card table and helping himself to a glass of milk and a blueberry muffin. "I'm eighteen dollars away from being able to get my catcher's mitt."

"Quite the capitalist, are you? How about I toss in an extra buck if you'll watch TV with Boris this morning, while I try to figure out how to work the modem on my computer?"

"I know how to work a modem," Joey said. "It's easy."

Diana stared at the boy in disbelief. "The instruction book is bigger than both Testaments of the Bible. I can barely figure out which cable to use." She grabbed the instruction book from the countertop and waved it in the air between them. "You need a Ph.D. in computer science to understand this blasted thing."

"Can I see?" asked Joey.

"Sure." Diana handed it to him. "I was going to offer it to Kath and Jenny as a high-tech coloring book, but reason got the better of me."

Diana watched while Joey munched blueberry muffins and thumbed through the manual.

"How many baud is your modem?"

It was the kind of question that usually got a man's face slapped, but fortunately, this time Diana recognized it as computerese.

"I don't know," she said, to Joey's amusement. "What's baud?"

Joey barely managed to withhold a sigh of disbelief. "How fast your modem can transfer information between computers."

"Oh." He told her how to track down the information in her equally weighty computer manual, and in a few moments she had the answer. "Twelve hundred," she said.

Joey nodded as if he'd expected as much, then ate a little more and read a little more. There must be a column in this, Diana thought as she watched him thumb through the pages. Certainly Mother could get a week's worth of material on computerese for the technically inept. Computers were as much a part of American life these days as VCRs and washing machines and—

"Okay," said Joey with a big grin. "I know how to hook it up."

Both the modem and her laptop computer were on the kitchen counter, and within minutes Joey had the computer talking to the modem and the modem wired up to the telephone, ready to transmit her priceless prose straight to the computer at her agent's office. Not that her agent didn't trust Diana to make her deadline, but the good woman had made it clear she would feel *much* more secure if she at least saw a chapter or two of Mother's latest work in progress.

"You're a genius, Joseph Marino," she declared when the boy had finished. "What on earth are they teaching kids at school these days—quantum physics?"

Joey shrugged his bony shoulders, as if technical wizardry were an everyday miracle. "I learned this at the hospital."

Some of Diana's high spirits flagged. "Quite a hospital," she said lightly. "I'm impressed. Were you rooming with a genius?"

"They had classes," he said, digging the toe of his Nike into the joint between two of the sand-colored floor tiles. "To keep us busy, you know."

"I think you deserve a raise."

His cheeks reddened. "Nah. Maybe a milk shake, though."

She lifted an eyebrow. "At nine in the morning?"

"Yeah. Chocolate, with lots of syrup."

"And whipped cream, I suppose."

"A ton of it."

"Your mother would shoot me, Joey."

"No, she wouldn't. She wants me to gain weight. She thinks I'm too skinny."

Diana was proud of the way she ignored the lump that was forming in her throat. "Okay, just this once. Computer geniuses deserve special treatment, I guess."

"Aw-right!" Joey hoisted himself up onto the counter and sat there, legs dangling, while she busied herself putting together the chocolate milk shake. His legs were dotted with Band-Aids and bruises and the other assorted badges of honor coveted by twelve-year-old boys, and if she didn't know better, it would be easy to imagine him racing around the dunes, scrambling through the brush, tossing his body at the waves and laughing as they tossed him back onto the shore.

"Are Kath and Jen real, real sick?" he asked as she scooped ice cream into the big Tupperware pitcher she was using as a makeshift, hand-operated blender.

"No, honey. Just bad colds, that's all."

He nodded, his legs swinging back and forth even faster. "Do they have to take a lot of medicines?"

She shook her head and added the chocolate syrup. "Baby aspirin, to bring the fever down."

He thought about that for a moment as she poured milk into the pitcher, then fastened the lid back on top. She'd raised the pitcher to shake the mixture, when he blurted out: "Do you think I'm going to die?"

Only her two college semesters of drama classes kept her from dropping the whole mess to the floor in shock. "Wh-what makes you ask that, Joey?" she managed, praying her face didn't betray the panic she was feeling.

"My mom thinks so," he stated. "I bet Gregory thinks so, too, but he won't talk about it. I wanted to know what you think."

"Well," she said carefully, "we all die sooner or later."

"That's not what I mean."

"I know that." Her eyelids fluttered closed for an instant, then she met his steady gaze. "I don't know enough about your condition to say, Joey." *I do know I want you to grow up to be an old, old man with a wife and children and grand-children all around you.*

"I think that's why Mom won't let me have one of Daisy's puppies," he confided as she poured the milk shake into a huge plastic cup. "I think she's afraid I'll die, and there will be nobody to love him."

"Oh, I don't know," she said, pouring herself a glass of orange juice and praying she'd say the right thing. "Your mom has an awful lot to do these days. Maybe a puppy just seems like too much to handle right now."

He shook his head. "I don't think that's the reason. I see the way she looks at me, real sad and angry—the same way she looked at Grandpa before he died."

"She loves you, Joey. It hurts her to see you feeling sick."

"I'm getting better. It's just the medicine making me sick, that's all."

"It can be pretty rough, can't it?" Diana commiserated, although God had seen fit to spare her firsthand knowledge.

"Yeah," Joey said matter-of-factly, "but I know I'm gonna be okay. Just wait and see."

"I will," she said, flashing him a bittersweet smile. "I want you to show me exactly how okay you're gonna be."

BY THE NEXT EVENING the twins' temperatures were back down to a steady 98.6, and Diana allowed them to watch TV in the solarium with Boris and Iggy for company. Paula had called a record eight times the day before, but since late the previous night the phone had been blessedly quiet.

Gregory had shown up at the door a little after six with ice cream for Kath and Jenny and a beautiful fresh fruit salad for Diana, in honor of the third—and hopefully, last—new start on her oft-postponed diet. "Help yourself," she'd said, flinging open the refrigerator to display a sinful array of cas-seroles, cakes and pasta specialties she'd put together to dou-ble-check her recipes. "What you can't eat, can go to Mary

Ann and Joey and Dave and Peggy, and anybody else you can think of.''

She had seriously underestimated Gregory's appetite, however, for by the time she popped a videocassette into the machine and settled down on the floor of the solarium to watch *Lady and the Tramp* with the twins, he had polished off more than half of the bounty and was making a gallant attempt at setting a new, world speed-eating record.

The girls were oohing and ahing over the restaurant scene as Lady and Tramp shared a romantic, spaghetti dinner, and Diana was doing her best not to let Gregory know she was misty-eyed.

"Disney was incredible," Gregory said, reaching for another helping of cold meat loaf. "Look at the color separations, will you?"

Diana nodded and prayed he wouldn't hear the sound of her sniffling.

"I read somewhere that each movement required hundreds of drawings." He shook his head and took another bite of food. "Unbelievable."

"Unbelievable," Diana echoed. *Unbelievable that a thirty-five-year-old woman would sit there, blubbering over the love story between a cocker spaniel and a mutt...*

"What was that?"

"I said, unbelievable."

He turned to look at her. "You're crying."

"No, I'm not."

"Look at me."

"So sue me." She ducked her head in embarrassment. "I'm a sucker for a love story."

"I'd hate to see you during *Gone with the Wind*."

She wiped at her eyes with the back of her hand and grinned up at him. "It's not a pretty sight."

His smile did wonderful things to her equilibrium. "I'll be the judge of that." He put his plate down and leaned back on the floor. "Come closer."

She hesitated, then slid across the polished wood until she

was right next to him. He draped his arm around her shoulders and she leaned into him, conscious of the play of his taut muscles against her side and the faint scent of sun and soap that always lingered with him. The girls giggled as the celluloid dogs slurped their spaghetti, and Ignatius cast them a baleful look as he moved his bulk to a position on the other side of the room.

"Women and children first!" screeched Boris, hopping from perch to perch. "Abandon ship!"

Gregory laughed out loud. "That's a new one. Where'd he get that from?"

"I rented *A Night to Remember*," said Diana, cuddling against him as easily as if she'd been doing so for years. "He thinks this is the Titanic, and Iggy's manning the lifeboats."

"Between that and the song from *Mr. Rogers's Neighborhood*, Laurence is in for a few surprises when he gets back."

"Shh," said Diana. "Let's not talk about that." This wasn't the time to talk about endings, not when she felt as if her life was opening up before her like a glittering Christmas present waiting to be unwrapped. "August will be here soon enough."

"Things don't have to end in August, Diana." His words were low, for her alone. "We have to talk about—" He stopped, tilting his head slightly to his left. "Did you hear that?"

"I didn't hear anything," she said, then heard the faint chiming of the doorbell. *Go away. Whoever you are, go away!*

"Answer the door," Boris commanded. "Dingdong. Dingdong. Avon calling."

"Maybe it's Mary Ann," Diana said, wishing whoever it was would go away. "Maybe Joey left something behind today."

"It better not be M.A. I'll fire her on the spot."

The doorbell sounded again.

"I'd better answer it," Diana said. "Maybe it's important."

Gregory was muttering something about getting a doorbell answering machine as Diana got to her feet and headed for the foyer and the front doors. Talk about rotten timing. She intended to dispatch this unexpected visitor in record time and get back into the solarium, before the twins had a chance to create any more mischief—or Gregory had a chance to change his mind.

Fixing her best we-don't-want-any look on her face, she opened the door—and found herself face-to-face with her sister.

Chapter Fifteen

"I don't believe it!" Diana stared at the woman on the front step. "You're in Monte Carlo."

"Not anymore," said Paula as Art climbed out of the car in the driveway. "I had to see my babies."

"Don't blame me," Art called out as he approached. "I thought I'd be gambling at the casino tonight."

Paula pushed her way past Diana into the foyer. "Where are they?"

"In the solarium."

"In the solarium! They're sick. They should be in bed."

"They're fine, Paulie. Their fevers are gone. If you'd called me, I would have told you."

Paula's mouth dropped open as she gazed around the huge, sunlit foyer and at the ocean that was visible through the French doors at the end of the house. "I don't believe this place! It's incredible."

"Empty," said Diana, aiming a look at Art, "but incredible." She headed toward the solarium. "Come on. I'll take you to your kids."

Diana knew she should be ashamed of herself, but took a fiendish delight in the fact that Kath and Jenny were more interested in Tramp's run from the dogcatcher than in their mother's sudden reappearance.

"I don't blame them," said Art, shaking hands with Gregory. "Right now, I'm not that happy to see Paula, either."

Paula dithered and fussed over the girls, who finally gave her offhanded kisses, then turned their attention back to the television program.

"To be or not to be," said Boris, training his beady eyes on Paula. "Only her hairdresser knows for sure...."

"Nasty old bird," Paula muttered. "That commercial hasn't been on in years."

Paula did, however, recover her good humor when Diana introduced her to Gregory. Diana found herself crossing her fingers behind her back that her sister wouldn't say anything embarrassing, but Paula was so preoccupied with the apparent loss of her children's esteem that meddling in Diana's romance wasn't uppermost in her mind.

"They hate me," Paula said woefully. "In just a few weeks, they've turned against me." She launched into a mass of psychobabble that made it difficult for Diana to keep a straight face.

"They're watching *Lady and the Tramp*," Diana said. "They wouldn't care if you were Big Bird himself, right now."

"Easy for you to say," Paula said, sniffling. "You're not their mother."

Art looked over at his tiny daughters, and a grin split his deeply tanned face. "You did a good job, Diana. The girls look pretty healthy to me."

"They *are* healthy," Diana said. "Their temperatures are normal and their appetites are back." She cast a quick glance at Gregory, but his handsome face was blandly pleasant. "You really didn't have to come home, guys."

"Tell that to my wife," Art said. "Wild horses couldn't have kept her away."

"I feel like a fool," Paula said. "All the terrible things I said to you, Diana. You've done a wonderful job with the girls." Her children taken care of, Paula now turned to the next topic at hand. When her eyes rested once again on Gregory, Diana nearly stopped breathing. "Dr. Stewart, are you—?"

Art unceremoniously clapped a hand over his wife's mouth. "The motor's running, Paula. Let's grab the girls' gear and get moving."

Paula squirmed out of his grasp. "Then turn off the engine. As long as we're here, I want to catch up on everything Diana's been up to."

"I meant the *helicopter's* engine."

"Helicopter?" Diana whistled in appreciation. "Haven't we come up in the world!"

"Wait'll I explain this one on my expense account. I said it was a family emergency."

"It could have been," said Paula. "They could have been raging with fever."

"This argument's costing me ten dollars a minute, Paula."

"Call the airport," Paula suggested, as Diana barely suppressed her groan of disappointment. "We can stay here tonight."

Art looked at his wife, then he looked at Diana and Gregory. "Not on your life, Paula. Let's pack the kids' stuff and get back to New Jersey."

I'm going to remember you in my will, Art Bradley, Diana vowed as she helped gather together the twins' paraphernalia. *You are a brother-in-law without equal.* She even made the requisite noises about vacating Gull Cottage for them since it was Art, after all, who was footing the bill. But he would have none of it, and she quickly gave up the fight. Gregory was quiet, but extraordinarily efficient, as he helped carry the table and chairs and double stroller out to the car; once Diana thought she saw a wily grin light up his face as he talked to Art beneath the porte cochere.

"Oh, my God!" The realization of what Paula's unexpected arrival meant, hit Diana with the force of a hurricane blowing in off the ocean. She'd been enjoying days of breathless anticipation, heightened by the fact that until the twins were gone, nothing more would happen. Without the girls there as a buffer, there was nothing stopping Diana from taking the next step in her relationship with Gregory Stewart.

There would be no one to interrupt them, no little faces popping up in the room when they shouldn't, no tender sensibilities to worry about.

Moonlight kisses. Slow dancing. Hot sun, cool nights, the promise of erotic splendor.

Now the twins were leaving, and in a few moments there would be only Diana and Gregory, alone together in the vastness of Gull Cottage.

And what happened next, she knew, would change her life forever.

PAULA KISSED DIANA on the cheek, then trained her best smile on Gregory. "And you make certain that Di brings you out to the house for dinner, Dr. Stewart. You did so much for her and my girls. I just don't know how to thank you."

Gregory was scrupulously polite, exceedingly charming, and—to Diana's practiced eye—more nervous than he had a right to be. "They're good kids," he said, shaking Paula's hand, then Art's. "Glad I could help."

"One more goodbye and we qualify for the Guinness Book of Records," Art said, putting his arm around his wife's shoulders and propelling her out the front door. "Enjoy the rest of the month."

Diana and Gregory stood on the top step and waved as the Bradley family disappeared down the driveway in their rented Mercedes. The only sounds were the crunching of the tires in the gravel and the loud sobbing of the twins.

"I don't think the girls wanted to go home," Diana said, as they went back inside and closed the door.

"Can you blame them?" Gregory asked. "They were having the time of their lives here."

"I'm going to miss them," she said, suddenly shy and nervous and wishing she had jumped into the Mercedes with Kath and Jenny. "This place will seem empty without them." She looked down at the ground and saw a tiny, red sneaker. "Kath's shoe," she said, bending to pick it up.

"Maybe if we jump into the car, we could catch up with them and—"

He took the shoe from her and dropped it back onto the floor. "No," he said, his voice low.

"No?" Her own voice was high and abnormally tight.

"No." He stepped toward her and her heartbeat accelerated. "It's too late now."

Her words died in her throat as he gently touched her cheek. The feelings that sprang to life inside her breast were an odd blend of the familiar and the exotic. She felt as if she'd always known him, had always been moving toward this moment in time; and yet as he drew her into his arms, she found herself trembling on the brink of unknown delights.

"It's not the end of the month yet," she said, when she found her voice again.

"We've waited long enough, Diana."

"I don't take this lightly," she said, knowing she risked shattering the fantasy that was blossoming around them. "I'm looking for more than a night—"

He kissed her with a tenderness that turned desire into something so much more wonderful. "What I feel for you isn't about one night, Diana." His steady gaze held her in thrall. "I think you know that."

"I know how it is for me, but—"

He took her hand and placed it against his chest, where she could feel the rapid pulsing of his heart. "Let's take the first step, Diana. Let me love you."

"Yes," she said, surrendering. "Yes."

He swept her into his arms and carried her up the staircase, the way she'd imagined a thousand times he would, in her most secret fantasies. Moving with powerful grace, he strode down the hallway as if Diana was no burden at all. As if she was precious, desired, valued beyond price.

As if she belonged to him.

The master bedroom was bathed in the violet hues of dusk; even the pale pink walls took on a faint amethyst tone. The girls' beds were pushed against the far wall and Ignatius, who had been curled up on the windowsill, sauntered from the room, meowing his displeasure.

"Not exactly like the movies, is it?" she asked, as he carried her toward Cleopatra's barge-bed.

"Movies aren't real life," he said, stopping at the foot of the platform ladder. "Movies don't last forever."

"This is where it gets complicated," she said, so nervous that her lips began to tremble. The thought of undressing, then climbing the ladder in the nude was more than she could bear to contemplate; surely only a fireman could carry an adult female over his shoulder. "Do we stop here? Do we undress now, or once we're actually in bed? What if—"

He gently set her down before him. "We do what feels right, Diana. That's all there is to it."

She watched, spellbound, as he stripped off his shirt and kicked his shoes under the platform. She slid out of her sandals and followed him up the ladder to the vast mattress, where she'd spent so many solitary nights imagining this very moment.

But not even in her most elaborate romantic dreams had she imagined anything as glorious as reality. There, in his arms, she felt beautiful. She felt cherished. She felt as if all that had gone before had been nothing more than a wrinkle in time.

Somehow their clothing disappeared, drifting down to the floor in a slow-motion ballet. Gregory opened his arms to her and she went to him freely, joyously, certain that she was where she wanted to be.

LATER ON, when the moon rode high over the ocean and the room was as dark as the night sky, it occurred to both of them that more had happened in that vast bed than simply the coming together of a man and a woman. Friendship had grown from desire; desire had blazed within friendship. They no longer knew which had come first; they no longer cared. A pledge had been made—albeit unspoken—and both Greg-

ory and Diana had the sense that their futures had been ir-
revocably joined from the first moment they met.

"It doesn't seem possible that it was less than three weeks
ago," Diana said, trailing a hand along the flat plane of his
belly. "Right now, I find it difficult to believe there was ever
a time when I didn't know you."

"So do I." Gregory gently cupped a breast in the palm of
one hand. "Imagine; we owe it all to a wrong turn in Riverhead."

She sighed as a voluptuous wave of pleasure shimmered
through her. "I love Riverhead. No wonder it's the county
seat." She propped herself up on an elbow and looked him
in the eye. "Come on," she urged. "You can tell me: what
did you think when we first met?"

"The truth?"

"I wouldn't expect less from you."

"I thought you were a cute little blonde who—"

"You thought I was a *what*?"

"A cute little blonde, with a fat cat and two kids and an
extremely lucky husband."

"So you did think I was married." She knew the post-
liberated woman in her should be annoyed by the phrase
"cute little blonde," but at that moment—eight and a half
pounds over her fighting weight—she found it pretty endearing.

He nodded. "The evidence pointed that way."

She flashed him a saucy grin. "Were you disappointed?"

"You didn't let me finish. I also thought you were flaky,
argumentative, and probably the most disorganized woman
I'd ever met."

"But of course, now you know better."

He grinned back at her. "Of course." He stroked her
shoulder, the curve of her breast. "I also wished I had a more
liberal attitude on wife-snatching."

"Don't you want to know what I thought about you?"

"I'm afraid to ask."

"Arrogant. Aggressive." She paused for effect. "And absolutely gorgeous."

"Yeah?"

She kissed him soundly. "Yeah."

"A sex object?"

She kissed him again. "Definitely."

"Should I be insulted?"

"Only if you don't like this...." She ran her hands across the muscles of his chest. "And this...." Her hands trailed lower. "Or this." Her hands moved lower still.

He exhaled on a rush of pleasure and leaned back against the pillow. "Being a sex object isn't all that bad."

"Dr. Stewart," she said, as her lips followed the trail her hands had blazed, "you haven't seen the half of it."

BRR-INGG.

"Hi...this is Paula.... We got home safely.... The girls miss you already.... Diana...? Where are you...? Pick up the phone, Diana.... I know you must be there.... Where are you...? Come on, Di, it's the middle of the night.... The least you can do is...Art...! Don't take that phone away from me.... Art!"

Click.

Good night, Paula.

DIANA HAD NEVER thought of herself as an intensely sexual woman, but apparently she had a great deal to learn about her true nature.

They didn't make love in the solarium—who knew what incriminating phrases Boris would pick up?—but it seemed to Diana that they made love in every other room of Gull Cottage that weekend.

Gregory was as inventive as he was passionate, taking her on a trip deep into erotic territory hitherto uncharted by either of them. Her normal caution didn't stand a chance against the fierce blaze of desire his touch ignited inside her heart. The next few days were a blur of sensation; his blue-green eyes dark with hunger; the intoxicating smell of his skin; the slippery feel of their bodies as they came together in the summer heat; the sound of the ocean crashing against the shore, providing a counterpoint to the wild pounding of their blood.

It wasn't until Sunday night, as they ate supper on the deck and watched the sky turn rose and indigo, that she remembered it all would end, once the month was over.

"You're quiet," Gregory said as she brought out the coffee and placed it on the small table between them. "Something wrong?"

She hesitated a moment, then decided anything less than full honesty was unfair to them both. "Time is racing by. In less than two weeks I'll be heading back home." *And where exactly is that?* she wondered. A motel? Paula's house? The back of her rented station wagon?

"I know," he said, pouring cream into his coffee and settling back against the railing. "The same thought occurred to me."

A deep sigh escaped her lips, but fortunately it was quickly carried away on the ocean breeze.

"In one month I'll be heading for the Caribbean," he said.

"I know," Diana answered. "That thought occurred to me, too."

"Seems like we have a problem, doesn't it?"

She shrugged in an attempt to look casual and unconcerned. "No strings," she said lightly. "We both knew it from the start."

His answer was both pithy and eloquent. "Forget the old rules, Diana. This is something neither one of us expected."

Her heart thudded violently inside her chest. "Meaning?"

"You're not leaving here on August 1."

"I'm not? Try telling that to Mrs. Geller."

He put down his coffee on the railing and pulled her into his arms. "I don't give a damn about Mrs. Geller. I'm telling you, you're not leaving."

"What about the new tenants? I can't just decide to commandeer Gull Cottage for another month.'' *Besides, I already tried!*

"You're staying with me."

"At the animal hospital?'' Not that staying there would bother her. She would stay in a shack, if it meant being with Gregory a little bit longer.

"On my boat. I took a slip a few miles from here. I'm bringing her down on the thirtieth."

Two extra weeks with him. It wasn't long enough—a lifetime wouldn't be long enough—but she had no intention of leaving paradise a second sooner than necessary.

"Say yes, Diana,'' he urged. "Give us the time to see if this is real."

He moved against her, all male dominance and power, and she fell, helpless before the flame. "Yes,'' she said as she gave herself up to him. "Yes."

Chapter Sixteen

"Hello, stranger." Mary Ann Marino waved at Gregory from behind the reception desk on Monday morning. "Long time no see."

"I can't take a long weekend now and then, M.A.?" There was nothing on heaven or earth that could have pulled him from Diana's side. Those first few days had been more like a honeymoon than simply the start of a love affair; the feeling of permanence, of union, had made it difficult for him to leave her this morning. Who would have figured that Gregory Stewart, the last of the loners, would surrender so completely—or feel so wonderful about it?

"A long weekend? You're going to be taking three *months* off, the end of next month. What was this, a practice session?"

"I took the boat out."

"And—?"

"And what? I had a few things to check out."

Mary Ann rolled her eyes toward the ceiling. Her teasing insistence continued. "I'll just bet you did."

"Why don't you mind your own business, M.A.? It might be good practice for you on your next job."

"You'd throw a single mother out on the street? What a rotten guy."

"You're too damn sure of yourself, that's your problem. You think you run this office."

"I *know* I run this office. Without me, you and Dave would drown in a sea of flea dip." She followed him back into his office cum temporary home. "So how serious is it, anyway?"

"I don't know what you're talking about."

"I know you too well for this dumb act, Gregory. You and Diana—what's the deal?"

"None of your business."

"Of course it's my business. I'm in favor of anything that keeps you in East Hampton a little longer."

"Don't get your hopes up. I'm still leaving, right on schedule."

Mary Ann's smile disappeared. "Doesn't sound like true love to me."

That's where you're wrong, M.A. What he felt for Diana was most definitely true love, high romance, any pop term you cared to put to it. Waking beside her each morning was like being a kid again on Christmas Day; he hadn't believed his heart was capable of such powerful, all-encompassing love.

However, the last thing he intended to do was give Mary Ann Marino any fuel for her fire. If he told his office administrator he was thinking of asking Diana to accompany him on his three-month sail to the Caribbean, Mary Ann would have a field day. The news would probably end up on the front page of the East Hampton *Star*.

Besides, first he had to ask Diana if she would go with him. But that was only a formality, because he had no intention of taking no for an answer.

Mary Ann grabbed his sleeve as he headed toward his office at the rear of the hospital. Her voice suddenly deepened. "I need a favor."

Gregory groaned and sat on the edge of her desk. "You took Daisy and her puppies of your own free will, M.A. No fair, backing out on it now." Joey had pleaded with his mother that Daisy looked lonely at the hospital with her three-week-old pups, and he'd persuaded a reluctant Mary

Ann to turn their house in Quogue into a canine nursery. "Which puppy are you going to keep?"

She didn't return his smile, and his gut tightened.

"I need a long lunch, Gregory."

"Joey?"

"Yeah."

"Take as long as you need." He flashed her another smile. "Better pick out a puppy soon, M.A., or you're going to end up with all of them."

"I'm worrying about my son," she snapped, "not a puppy. The doctors want him at the hospital."

"Joey's going to be fine," Gregory said, turning away. "I know it."

"You're not God," Mary Ann said as he headed toward his office. Her voice was as cold as glare ice. "You can't know who gets well and who doesn't. There's no guarantee Joey'll be as lucky as you were."

Shut up, he thought violently as he closed his office door behind him. *I don't want to hear it. I don't want to hear about luck and the odds and the hand of the Almighty picking and choosing his favorite sons.* He'd spent almost five years wondering why he'd been lucky—and wondering how long that luck would last. The thought that his luck might have tipped the odds against Joey Marino was more than he could stand.

Joey had stopped spending his days at Gull Cottage with Diana. Sure, they all used the girls' departure as a cover, but the real reason for his absence was painfully clear to anyone with eyes.

Gregory, however, was determined not to see any of it as he slipped into his lab coat and searched for his wayward stethoscope. The lure of the open sea grew more enticing with each day that passed, and it occurred to him more than once that waiting for August 15 to come around wasn't necessary, after all. This summer season had proved to be unusually slow. Except for Boris and his frequent cries for help, East Hampton's animal population was enjoying an enviable state of good health. Dave was back at work, and Charlie was set to join the staff full-time in less than ten days. Mary Ann kept the business side running smoothly. They might not notice he was gone, until he was halfway to Anguilla.

Which was all right with him, as long as he had Diana Travis by his side.

"OH, COME ON, DI!" Paula's amused laugh floated through the phone wires between East Hampton and Bernardsville, New Jersey. "Nobody's perfect. Not even Mr. Tall-Dark-and-Handsome."

"He is, Paulie. I'm telling you, this man *is* perfect," Diana stretched out on the chaise longue on the deck and lifted her face toward the morning sun. Amazing how quickly she'd grown accustomed to sun decks and solariums and having the Atlantic Ocean at her own back door.

"No bad habits?"

"None that I've noticed." Paula's disbelief was quite delightful. "He doesn't smoke. He drinks moderately. He doesn't chew his nails or snore or leave the toilet seat up. What more can a woman ask for?"

"Did you say 'snore?' "

"You were paying attention."

"Have you—?"

"Draw your own conclusion."

"I can't believe it," said Paula. "You really did it."

Diana laughed at the shock in her sister's voice. "I'm thirty-five years old, Paulie. It shouldn't be that much of a surprise."

"I'm talking about your plan. You did it, Di, just the way you said you would. You found the perfect man—and ahead of schedule, at that."

"Slow down, big sister. I think you're getting ahead of yourself."

"Can you tell me it's not serious?"

Diana fell quiet. "No," she said after a moment. "I can't."

"What happens after July 31, when the lease on Gull Cottage is up?"

"We've talked about that."

"And?"

"And none of your business, Paulie," she said gently. She loved her sister dearly, but wasn't about to tell Paula about Gregory's invitation to spend two weeks on his boat. Big-sisterly advice wasn't what Diana needed at the moment.

"When are you coming home?"

"Home?" Diana laughed. "Where's home? I'm footloose and fancy-free, and able to hang my hat anywhere I choose."

"Are you moving in with him?"

"You're pushing, Paula."

"Come on, Di, what's the deal? Are there wedding bells in the air?"

"You'll be the first to know." She certainly couldn't tell Paula that she had the feeling Gregory would be asking her to sail to the Caribbean with him come mid-August, because if she did, her sister would be on her way to the printer for engraved wedding invitations.

"There has to be a catch someplace," said Paula. "Nobody gets everything they want in life—not even you."

"Why is happiness so hard to understand?"

"I suppose next thing I know, you'll tell me you're pregnant, right on schedule. Mother becomes a mother."

Diana laughed delightedly at the thought of children with Gregory's beautiful, blue-green eyes. "You know me, Paulie: I'm the General's daughter, through and through." How wonderful that this serendipitous detour to East Hampton had given her the man of her dreams. She would have to remember to send Paula and Art a magnum of champagne and her undying gratitude.

"Be careful, kiddo," said Paula. "Just remember, no one's perfect."

"I'll remember."

"But you won't believe it, will you?"

"No," said Diana, thinking about Gregory Stewart. "Not for a minute."

THEY WENT to see Joey at the hospital that evening after supper. It was obvious he wanted very much to talk to Gregory alone, and twice Diana excused herself, so they could have some privacy. Each time, however, Gregory made a point of drawing her into the conversation in a way that made it awkward—if not impossible—to get away.

Mary Ann's mother came in a little after seven to visit her grandson, and Gregory eagerly snatched that opportunity for them to say their goodbyes, right in the middle of Mrs. Gallagher's plans for her grandson's birthday party in mid-August.

"We'll come by tomorrow," Diana said, kissing the boy on the forehead and smiling as he turned bright red. "Maybe I'll even challenge you to a game of gin rummy, if you're up to it."

Joey mumbled his thanks and looked up at Gregory, his dark brown eyes questioning. But Gregory merely gave him an awkward pat on the shoulder and said, "Later, pal." He was out of the room and down the corridor before Joey could even say goodbye.

The setting sun cast a violent, reddish-orange glow across the asphalt parking lot. Gregory sprinted toward the Corvette, and Diana found herself breaking into a run to keep up with him.

"Slow down," she called out. "My sandals aren't made for the hundred-yard dash. What's wrong with you, anyway?"

If he heard her, he gave no notice of it. By the time she reached the sports car, he had the passenger door unlocked and was on his way around to the driver's side. A feeling of foreboding settled across Diana's shoulders like a breeze off Long Island Sound.

"Let's take the boat out," he said after he started the engine. "We'll shoot out to the marina and be there in no time."

"Isn't it a little late for a pleasure cruise?" she asked, trying to keep the anxiety from her voice.

"Moonlight on the Sound is a sight to behold."

She knew he meant it as a seductive invitation, but his words held a curiously flat tone, and her apprehension escalated. "I don't exactly feel like a romantic evening. I'm worried about Joey."

"Don't be." Gregory gunned the Corvette's engine, then shifted into reverse and backed out of the parking spot. "He's going to be fine."

They rode in silence, broken only by the low sounds of music from the car's stereo system. Not even Marvin Gaye— or the beautiful scenery rolling past her window—were enough to lift Diana's spirits. Her heart ached for Joey, for what he was going through in that hospital. She knew that neither she nor Gregory could do anything to help banish his disease, but what they could do was help keep his morale from flagging. The only problem was, that couldn't be done from the front seat of Gregory's Corvette as it sped toward the marina.

Paula had said that nobody was perfect. Maybe Gregory was hospital-phobic, one of the millions of Americans whose knees turned to Jell-O the moment they saw a gurney or an IV.

She glanced over at him and felt a rush of love race through her. One *tiny* flaw, and a curable one at that.

99.9% perfect was still pretty darned impressive.

They made it to the marina in record time. Before Diana knew it she was on the boat, and Gregory had cast off toward the shoreline of Connecticut across the Sound. The only sound was that of the boat's engine. The night breezes were soft and gentle and cool, an odd counterpoint to the tension in the air between them. After they had put some distance between themselves and the marina, she walked over to where he stood alone at the wheel, seemingly faraway in thought, and placed her hand against his back.

"What is it?" she asked quietly. "Can I help you?"

He cut the engine and dropped anchor. "Yes," he said, sweeping her into his arms. "You're the only one who can."

He dipped his head toward her, and in the next instant found her mouth and possessed it. His tongue demanded entry and quickly drew her into a silent, sensual battle that made her blood run hot and quick. He stood with his legs spread wide, drawing her up against him until that part of him that was hard and male and hungry was the only reality in her rapidly shifting world. She felt weak with longing, burning from within, hollow and aching and yearning to be filled.

He slid her skirt up her thighs, then with one quick movement tore the lace panties from her hips. She moaned as he found her with his fingers, and a dizzying wave of sensation threatened to destroy what was left of her equilibrium.

"Go with it," he murmured into her ear. "Give over, Diana."

His words were all she needed to send her crashing over the edge of the precipice, and she moved shamelessly, wantonly against his hand as he held her tight against him.

"My knees are weak," she whispered as the last wave of sensation ebbed.

"I'll take care of that." She heard the rasp of metal, followed by the slither of cloth falling to the deck; in the next instant his hands were around her waist and she was lifted up, as easily as if she were made of gossamer and silk.

"We're not finished yet," he said, his voice low.

"I was hoping you'd say that," she managed as, to her amazement, desire coiled within her again.

Slowly he lowered her, inch by agonizing inch, until he rested against the place where she was hot and moist and ready.

"Now?" he asked, throbbing against her.

"Oh, God, yes...."

It was a long time before they spoke again.

TELL HER, Gregory thought, as he looked at Diana dozing in his arms later on. *Do it now, before it's too late.*

It seemed to him that their relationship was advancing by quantum leaps. In less than one month—a blink of an eye in the scheme of things—they had moved from being strangers to friends to lovers as naturally as drawing their next breath. Neither one doubted the depth and power of the bond that had inexplicably joined them. In a perfect world, that would be more than enough for a lifetime.

The world wasn't perfect, however, and neither was he. He was scared and angry, and he wished he didn't have to tell her anything at all, that he could go on pretending he was the perfect man with the perfect body and the perfect life—and the most singularly perfect chance at happiness with the woman of his dreams.

Unfortunately, they both deserved better. Damn it, he'd seen her with Joey, he'd seen the compassion and unflinchingly honest way she'd handled the boy. She hadn't been repelled by his illness; she hadn't fawned over him or made Joey feel anything less than the terrific person he was. Diana had the gift of understanding, and a talent for loving that was as deeply maternal as it was mysteriously female.

But Gregory was a man, not a twelve-year-old boy. Maternal affection wasn't what he was after—not by a long shot. He wanted the deep, passionate love they'd found to last; the powerful, transcendent miracle of two adults freely choosing to come together in love and desire. He couldn't promise her children; he couldn't promise her that he wouldn't one day again be faced by disease. Those promises were not his to make.

All he could do was promise to love her and cherish her as long as he lived, and pray that that would be enough.

WHEN DIANA WOKE UP in his cabin later on, Gregory was leaning back against the headboard, watching her. His chest was bare, and his tanned skin stood out in sharp contrast to the stark whiteness of the sheets.

"Hi," she said, pushing her hair away from her eyes. "Can't sleep?"

He shook his head, still watching her. "I didn't try."

She scooted closer to his side, reveling in the heat emanating from his skin and the hypnotic rocking of the boat. "I slept wonderfully."

He chuckled and drew her into an embrace, so that her cheek rested against the hard muscle of his shoulder. "Dream of me, I hope?"

"I dreamed of you and the twins playing catch on the beach." She pressed a kiss to his chest. "You would make a wonderful father. You—" She sensed rather than felt him tense and pull away from her touch. "Is something wrong?"

"We need to talk."

Her heart hammered a deep and painful rhythm inside her chest. "Talk?" she asked, forcing a lightness into her voice. "There are much better things to do than talk, Gregory." She let her fingers trail down his belly, but he took her hand in his and held it tight.

"There's something I have to tell you," he continued, his tone dark as the night beyond the porthole. "I wasn't going to, but it occurred to me that it isn't fair to either of us if I don't." Tears stung behind her eyelids, and she tried to pull away from him, but his grip was unyielding. "I've waited long enough. I owe you this much."

Oh, dear God, she thought, wildly searching about for a way to escape. *Don't tell me you're in love with someone else...not now, when you've come to mean so much to me.* One week ago she might have been able to pick up the pieces and move on; now she knew he would be part of her forever, no matter what happened.

Summoning up every ounce of courage at her command, she met his eyes. "What is it?"

His gaze darted from the porthole to the narrow closet,

then finally settled reluctantly upon her. "I owe you an explanation."

"You don't owe me anything, Gregory. All you owe me is—"

"Quiet," he said, pressing a hand against her mouth. "Don't make this any harder than it already is."

"You're scaring me, Gregory. What on earth is wrong?" *Are you a spy? Are you a mad scientist? A movie actor's child or deposed potentate? Tell me, damn you, Gregory Stewart!* Say something, to rid her of the feeling that her entire life was about to be blown to kingdom come.

He took a long breath; his heart beat wildly beneath her icy hands. "Joey isn't the only one with cancer, Diana. I had it, too."

The words tumbled in her brain like vending machine ice cubes sliding into a paper cup, and the sudden rush of cold that swept over her made it difficult to think with anything resembling clarity. "I—I don't understand. You're the picture of health," she said, hoping to erase the words before they took permanent shape in her brain. *I don't want to hear this, Gregory. Don't tell me I'm going to lose you....*

"You should have seen me five years ago," he said. "It wasn't a pretty sight."

She looked at his body, at the beautiful plane of his flat belly, the swell of musculature, and found it impossible to imagine anything but splendor. "I don't see any scars, Gregory. You look perfect to me."

"They're there, believe me. Just faded."

"I don't understand."

"Hodgkin's."

"Dear God, Gregory...I didn't know."

"That's the point. You weren't supposed to."

"Are you—? Will you...?" Her words trailed off in an awkward mumble. What on earth would Mother recommend in a situation like this?

"It was rough," he said, his tone matter-of-fact, "but I hung in. September 1 I get the all clear."

"And then you can be sure you're fine?" She was desperate for reassurance. "Then you can be positive?"

He took her face into his hands and looked into her eyes. "Even then I don't come with a guarantee. I want you to understand that."

"But the all clear—what does that mean?"

"It's a nominal goal. Five years with no visible signs of disease mean you have a better than good chance of avoiding a recurrence."

Nobody comes with a guarantee, Diana. Nobody is perfect. Not you, not this man you love, not the nieces you adore or the sister who drives you crazy.

"Is this what happened with your fiancée?" she asked after a moment.

"Partly. Sick men weren't high on her list."

"You're better off," Diana said, anger heating her voice. "She was a fool."

"She was honest. She couldn't handle it and she walked. I can't fault her for that."

Diana's head pounded with a volatile mixture of outrage and fear; her heart ached with love and denial. "The words 'in sickness and in health' mean something, Gregory. It's part of the deal."

"That's why she didn't marry me, Diana. She knew she couldn't keep her end of the bargain."

"Fool," she said, kissing his shoulder, the juncture between shoulder and arm, the hard wall of his chest. "Nothing will ever happen to you." *I won't let it. I've waited too long to find you, to love you.* "I can't imagine life without you."

No wonder he'd been reluctant to visit Joey in the hospital. Joey's experience only pointed to the fact that he had yet to reveal his own brush with illness to Diana.

"You want children, don't you?"

She nodded, fear once again nipping at the edges of her mind. "Very much."

"I can't promise I can give you any."

"But there's still a possibility, isn't there? You *might* father a child?'' *Please, God, don't ask this of me. I want this man, his children....*

''Yes. Not probable, but still possible.''

''Medical science is amazing,'' she said, forcing herself to believe her own words. ''As long as we're both healthy, there will be a way,'' *I can handle this. There's in vitro fertilization, and surrogate sperm donors, and adoption. Look at how you love Kath and Jenny. It doesn't matter how the child arrives—all that matters is that you and Gregory love each other.*

''Mary Ann was right,'' he said, ruffling her curls. ''You're an incurable optimist.''

''Yes,'' she said fiercely, covering his body with hers. ''I am.'' Fever sizzled through her blood, a violent desire to affirm life in the most basic manner, and she understood what had driven Gregory earlier that evening.

She encircled his nipple in her mouth, drawing it against her teeth, sliding her tongue across the hard nub until his body began to move in an answering rhythm. Her thighs straddled his lean hips, and she felt him grow hard and powerful beneath her. Instantly she was ready for him, moist and pliant and aching to be filled; but that wasn't enough. That simple act of coming together couldn't possibly be enough.

What she wanted was to own him, to pour her own strength and hope and future into him, to burn away fear and pain and uncertainty with the white-hot fire that was building inside her.

What she wanted was to believe it would all work out, exactly as she had it planned.

Chapter Seventeen

Diana stood in the middle of a pile of boxes and held up her hands in submission. It was the morning of July 31, and once again she was behind schedule.

"Where did all of this come from?" she exclaimed with a groan. "How can one person accumulate so much junk in less than a month?"

Gregory picked up the largest of the boxes and pretended to stagger under its weight. "And I invited you to stay on my boat? I must have been nuts—we'll sink before we get five hundred feet away from the pier." Just that morning he had taken possession of a slip on the south shore until Labor Day, even though he intended to be gone before August was over.

"Having a change of heart, Dr. Stewart?"

He put the box down. "Never," he said, drawing her into his arms. "That's one thing that will never happen."

She glanced at his watch. "You'll be late for work," she said as he kissed the side of her throat. "You should—"

"Quiet," he said. "I'm my own boss, remember?"

She sighed with pleasure. "I remember."

"Once we board, I'm tossing all watches in the drink." He leaned back and met her eyes. "Think you can handle that, Mother?"

"No," she said, so quickly that they both laughed. "I'm not sure I can."

"You have a lot to learn about having fun." He ran his hands along the inward curve of her waist.

"And you have a lot to learn about—" She whispered a provocative suggestion into his ear.

"I think I'll call in sick."

She extricated herself from his embrace. "School's not in session this morning."

His eyes glittered with promise. "You'll pay for this."

"I was hoping you'd say exactly that." She waved him off to work and went back inside Gull Cottage to finish packing.

Diana found it hard to believe that three and a half weeks could cause such a sea change in her life, but there it was.

She had arrived at Gull Cottage on July 1, filled with plans for her great Labor Day husband hunt; she was leaving Gull Cottage with the man of her dreams. She might not have made all the progress on her manuscript that she would have liked, but she was certainly way ahead of schedule when it came to love and romance.

They hadn't spoken about his illness since the night he told her he'd had cancer. There seemed no need to dwell on the darker side of life; she had only to look at him to see he brimmed with health and vitality. And if sometimes at night—in the darkest hours before dawn—her mind turned to cancer and the specter of losing him one day, she was to be forgiven. The depressing thoughts always disappeared with the coming of daylight.

And although he had told her that fathering children would be a long shot for him, her mind had skittered over that fact and settled on the one chance in a hundred that it would happen someday.

Paula had said no one was perfect, and now Diana had reason to agree with her sister. Gregory wasn't perfect, but he still came closer to that sublime state than anyone she had ever known. He possessed a kindness, a compassion for living creatures—both for the two-and four-legged kind—that only made her love him more.

It was inevitable that they should always be together. She could feel it in her soul, each time they came together in that preposterous barge-bed at Gull Cottage. She believed in fate or destiny or karma, or whatever other name was currently being put to that odd sense of déjà vu that swept over her each time he took her into his arms.

They belonged together. They were right together. It was as simple as that.

The rest of the morning flew by in a blur of cardboard boxes, strapping tape and excitement.

"Who would have imagined it?" she asked Paula, when her sister called at the noon hour. "Just thirty days ago I was an overweight, unhappy divorcée."

"And now?" Paula prompted, her tone skeptical. "Last I knew, you were still a divorcée."

"But I'm happy," Diana said with a quick laugh. "And I think my divorcée days are numbered."

There was silence from Paula's end of the line.

"No congratulations, Paulie?"

"I'm in shock."

"You were the one who said I was ahead of schedule."

"Don't you think you may be moving too fast, Di?"

"Need I remind you of your own whirlwind courtship?" Diana countered.

"I'm the spontaneous one, remember? You're the careful one."

"I know what I'm doing, Paula." Gregory was the finest man she'd ever known, and the thought of spending the rest of her life with him made her glow with pleasure.

"Even though he has cancer?"

"*Had* cancer. He's fine."

"But children, Di. Are you forgetting how much you want children?"

Why on earth had she ever confided in her sister? "Things will work out," she said, tossing a stack of magazines into a cardboard box. "I didn't say he was sterile."

Her flighty sister was being strangely persistent. "Don't bank on miracles," Paula warned.

"I won't," said Diana, but of course, she was lying. She knew all about miracles. Wasn't it a miracle that Gregory had survived? Wasn't it a miracle she'd met him?

Was it so difficult to imagine that God had one more miracle tucked up his flowing sleeve and earmarked for them?

MIRACLES, unfortunately, were in short supply.

Diana and Gregory were enjoying a moonlight take-out dinner on the deck and watching the Atlantic crashing against the shore.

"I'm going to miss this view," Diana said with a sigh. "Look at the way the moonlight plays off the whitecaps."

"You'll have an even better view when we set sail." Gregory poured wine into their glasses and leaned back against the deck railing. "The sky is jet black and the stars twinkle like diamonds against it."

Her breath caught in her throat. "Are you—are you asking me to come with you?"

He reached over and took her hands in his. "Three months," he said. "Only the two of us and the open sea."

Let this be real. Let it be only the beginning of something strong and true.

"I don't know what to say. I wasn't expecting this, Gregory." *Wishing for it, dreaming of it, but certainly not expecting it.*

"Say the word, Diana, and we could be on our way by this time next week."

A thrill of excitement rippled through her. "I don't know.... This time next week?"

"It's up to you."

She hesitated. "What about Joey's birthday party? We did promise to be there—he worships the ground you walk on, Gregory." The boy's birthday was August 14, the day before Gregory was due to set out for the Caribbean, and she had assumed they would be part of the celebration.

Gregory turned and looked out toward the ocean. "His aunts are coming out for it and both of his grandmothers. He'll never notice we're not around."

"He'll notice. He—"

He leaped up, then drew her to her feet and into his arms. "Say yes, Diana. What are we waiting for? What's the point to hanging around, when we both know we want to take the next step? Let's get our life together started now."

She started to laugh, a high-pitched sound that sounded almost like a giggle. "You're mad, Gregory! Are you saying we should—?"

"Marry me." He swept her into his arms, the way he had that night he carried her up the staircase to the bed on the second floor. "Let's say the words, sign the documents, tie it all up legal and nice before we get any older."

"You *are* mad! I'm not going anywhere, Gregory. We have plenty of time for a big, church wedding with all the trimmings, after we—"

"We will do all of those things, but we'll do them later on. This wedding will be for us."

"We haven't known each other that long. We—"

He carried her through the open French doors and headed toward the legendary staircase in the center hall. "Last chance, Diana. Say yes, or I'll be forced to take you upstairs and use unlawful persuasion to get you to marry me."

She was laughing so hard that she could barely draw a breath, much less talk. "Unlawful persuasion sounds interesting. Why don't you—?"

Once again, the telephone interrupted them.

They looked at each other and groaned. "Paula," said Diana, shaking her head, as Gregory put her back onto her feet.

"That woman is uncanny." Gregory followed her into the kitchen. "There's one good reason for leaving now; she won't be able to find us at sea."

"You don't know my sister," said Diana over her shoulder. "She'll find a shortwave radio and have us flagged down by a passing cruise ship."

But it wasn't Paula. It was Mary Ann, and the news wasn't good.

NONE OF IT was real.

Not the stink of fear in the hospital corridor; not the soft, familiar sound of rubber-soled shoes in the halls; not the distant rumble of voices, as doctors played God and determined who would live and who would die.

Gregory saw and heard and smelled it all, but none of it penetrated. Adrenaline rocketed through his body, and all he could think of was flight. The wide door to the emergency room beckoned to him like Circe on the rocks, and the only thing that kept him seated on the hard, vinyl bench was Diana's hand gripping his. The words *critical* and *surgery* roamed the edges of his mind, but the reality of it refused to sink in.

None of this had anything to do with the Joey Marino he loved—or with Gregory himself. What in hell was he doing there? He'd been there five years ago, watched the doctors poke and prod, heard the awful, terrifying words, felt the darkness rising up, until he couldn't breathe or see, or hear anything but his own fear.

He should get up. He should walk toward that door and out of the hospital. There was nothing he could do for the boy, nothing anyone could do for the boy. It was in the hands of the doctors now—and God.

You're almost there, he told himself, chanting a litany to ease his pain. *You're almost there. Four more weeks and you'll have it made. None of this can ever touch you again.*

He looked over at Diana, at the gentle curve of her cheek and jaw, and forced himself to stay in his seat—for now.

She was free and he was free, and the open sea was theirs for the asking. There was no way he'd wait until the middle of August.

No way in hell.

SOMETHING was terribly wrong. Diana didn't need ESP to know that their trip to the hospital had gotten to Gregory, and when he finally grabbed her arm and said it was time to leave, she didn't argue. Mary Ann was surrounded by family and friends; she hugged Diana and Gregory and thanked them for being there, but the woman's mind was clearly on her son, so Diana felt comfortable about leaving.

What she didn't feel comfortable about was Gregory.

He almost vibrated with tension. His movements were faster, sharper; his grip on her hand as they crossed the parking lot was almost painful. Gregory was a man who'd had his fill of hospitals, and she couldn't blame him for wanting to escape as quickly as possible. Besides, it wasn't as if they were walking out on Joey. The first moment he was able to see visitors, Diana intended to be there, with bells on.

"Feel like stopping for anything?" Gregory asked as he headed the 'Vette back toward East Hampton.

Diana shook her head. "I know it's hard to believe, but I'm not hungry. If I'm ever going to get things packed into the station wagon before I leave tomorrow morning, we'd better get back to Gull Cottage."

They drove in silence through Quogue and past Southampton College, whizzing through Westhampton Beach until they finally passed the crystal-clear pond at the edge of the village of East Hampton. Gregory's tension filled the car, despite the way he tapped out a rhythm on the steering wheel.

This isn't about Joey. The thought sprang full-blown into her mind and took possession. *This is about us.*

He eased the sports car along the curving driveway and came to a stop beneath the shelter of the porte cochere. He cut the engine, and she was certain the sudden acceleration of her heartbeat was the loudest sound for miles.

Boris greeted them cheerfully, calling "Identify yourself, soldier!" while Ignatius entwined himself around Diana's ankles and meowed for food. Mechanically she made her way into the kitchen and prayed she hadn't packed away every last can of seafood supper. Gregory jumped right into carrying boxes out to the station wagon, leaving Diana alone with the cat—and a sense of unease that grew with each passing minute.

Finally she knew she would explode if she didn't confront him. She upended the cat food onto a paper plate, put it down for Iggy, then marched outside to the station wagon.

"What's wrong?" she demanded as Gregory slid one of her suitcases into the rear compartment. "You're making me a nervous wreck. Have you changed your mind about things?"

He brushed off his hands on the legs of his jeans and looked her right in the eye. "As a matter of fact, I have."

"Well," she said, clearing her throat as she struggled to seem calm and collected, "I guess it's better to find that out now, rather than once we're floating out there in the middle of nowhere."

"That's not what I'm talking about."

"It isn't?"

"No. I'm talking about leaving for the Caribbean."

She hadn't realized she had been holding her breath until then. "You had me going for a moment."

He touched her cheek. "It was unintentional."

She thought about Joey and the uncertainty of his situation. "I'm glad you feel the same way I do. Our plans don't seem right now, do they?"

"Not at all."

"I was going to bring up the subject myself, once we finished loading the station wagon." How could they blithely set sail for the Bahamas and points south, when the boy's future dangled on a fragile thread of hope?

"No time like the present."

She sighed with relief. "So we're not leaving next week."

"Not next week." His blue eyes sparkled with an almost dangerous light. "We're leaving tomorrow."

Chapter Eighteen

"Very funny." *A bad joke, but a joke, nevertheless.* Diana started back toward the house. "Let's finish up the coffee before I clean up the kitchen."

Gregory closed the rear compartment of the station wagon and caught up with her at the front door. "I wasn't kidding."

"Of course you were," she said as they entered the front hall. "You don't just head off to the Caribbean on twelve hours' notice."

He snapped his fingers. "Why not?"

"Okay, joke's over, Gregory. How do you want your coffee?"

"To go," he said, trying to make her laugh. "Same way you should have yours."

Dear God, she thought, her anxiety returning like the incoming tide. *He's serious. He means every single word....*

Once in the kitchen she busied herself searching the cupboards for Styrofoam cups and pulled the milk container from the almost empty refrigerator, while he watched her from the entrance.

"What about my deadline?" she asked lightly, handing him a cup of coffee.

"You told me you could finish up anywhere."

"That was before I knew you were taking off August 1."

"Don't worry," he said, flashing that manic grin again. "We'll find you a mailbox."

"That's not what worries me, Gregory."

"We already know you don't get seasick."

"Gregory, I—"

"We can get a head start on hurricane season."

"Damn it, Gregory!" she exploded. "What about Joey?"

He broke eye contact for a split second, then looked back at her. "What about him?"

"Don't," she warned, her voice low. "Don't play games, not with this."

His expression didn't waver. "The kid's in good hands. There's nothing we can do to help him."

"We can be there for moral support."

His laughter was short and harsh. "Like I said, there's nothing we can do to help him."

"He looks up to you."

"He has his mother and his family."

"His mother and his family haven't been through it, Gregory. You have."

Again he looked away for a moment. "Doesn't make a hell of a lot of difference, Diana. Not when you come down to it."

"It makes a difference to Joey. If you can get through it, so can he."

"I'm not through it yet."

"In four weeks or so, you will be."

"In four weeks or so I'll be sunning on a beach in Anguilla."

"I'm all in favor of sunning on a beach, but I don't see why we have to set sail tomorrow."

"You're not listening, Diana. It's not up for debate. We leave in the morning."

"Don't push me, Gregory." Her voice was still low, but its tone almost defiant now. "I've already given up more—" She stopped, horrified by the words she'd almost spoken. *I've already given up having children of my own with you.*

"Don't censor yourself on my account. Tell me everything

you've given up for me. Tell me how tough it is to live with
cancer. Go ahead, Diana. Tell me the whole damned thing.''

"Yes," she snapped, "It *is* hard, but that's not what this
is about.''

He folded his arms across his chest and leveled his steady,
dispassionate gaze at her. "The hell it isn't. It always comes
down to that in the end.''

"Okay, you want to hear it, I'll tell you. I don't want to
love you, then lose you, but I'm willing to take the risk.''

"How compassionate," he drawled.

Her hand itched for contact with the sharp angle of his
cheekbone. "You're going too far, Gregory. This isn't a
joke.''

"If you'll take note, I'm not laughing.''

She took a deep breath and tried again. "You can't leave
Joey now, right before surgery. It isn't right.''

"Staying around isn't going to make a difference.''

"Are you so selfish that you can't understand that the boy
loves you? That he needs you for moral support? The simple
fact that you've made it has to make him feel better.''

"Is this some more of Mother's free pop psychology?''

She raised her arm to slap him, but he caught her wrist
and held it fast.

"I wouldn't," he warned.

She didn't. He released her hand, and she jammed it into
the pocket of her trousers.

"Smart move." He leaned against the kitchen counter.
"An even smarter move would be admitting the real problem.''

"More pop psychology, *Dr.* Stewart?''

He let her volley pass unanswered. "You don't get guar-
antees in life, Diana.''

"I never asked for any.''

"I'm leaving tomorrow.''

She noted the rock-hard set of his jaw and wondered if
she'd ever really known him at all. He was as far removed
from the kindhearted man who'd helped change the girls'

diapers as Diana was from her sister. "I think you should stay until Joey gets through surgery."

"With or without you," he said, his voice low and terrifyingly controlled. "I'll be gone before the day is out."

"Then you'll be going without me." Her voice was as controlled as his; she marveled at her capacity for deception.

"Then I'll be going without you. If you can't deal with my situation the way it is, you might as well get out now."

"I guess that's it, then," she said, wondering if the sound of her heart breaking could be heard in the quiet kitchen.

"I guess it is.".

She thought of Joey Marino and the look in his big, brown eyes when he was with Gregory. "For Joey," she urged, trying one last time. "If you leave tomorrow, you aren't being fair to him."

The set of his jaw didn't soften. "If I stay, I'm not being fair to me."

"So you're not perfect," she said with a shake of her head. "You're a bastard, like everyone else."

"I'm human, just like everyone else. Maybe that's what you can't handle." He turned and headed toward the front door with Diana close behind.

"Think about this, Dr. Stewart," she said as he opened the door wide. "Maybe it wasn't cancer that drove your fiancée away. Maybe it was you."

"And maybe you'd better think about this. All of your homegrown remedies can't change the fact that this situation is out of your control, and now, so am I."

He turned and disappeared down the steps. Moments later she watched as the taillights of the Corvette moved down the curving driveway.

"All's well that ends well," called Boris from the solarium.

Not this time, Boris. Not this time at all.

IT TOOK GREGORY most of the night to finish transferring his gear to the boat. By dawn he had cleared out the room at the back of his office and polished off the rest of the paperwork on his desk. A stack of checks was signed and ready to be deposited, all he had left to do was transfer part of his profits into his personal account when the bank opened, and he'd be ready to go.

He heard the sound of a car engine close by, but ignored it. Fool that he was, he'd spent the better part of the night listening for the rumble of Diana's rented station wagon, waiting for her to show up with her cat and her computer and her stacks of boxes, eager to apologize and ready to go.

It hadn't happened.

But then, he'd never been much of a believer in fantasy.

Although the trappings were different, Diana was no different than Hayley. Neither woman had been good at dealing with uncertainty; both had chosen the easy way out. He just hadn't expected it from Diana.

To hell with her, he thought, gulping some coffee from a 7 Eleven cup. What did he need with Diana and her Pollyanna view of life that turned dark at the first brush with reality? It was his life they were talking about, his decision. If he wanted to sail to the Caribbean, he'd sail to the Caribbean.

Joey would be fine. It was a setback, that was all, and a minor setback at that. Three months from now, when he sailed back up the wintry coast to East Hampton, the kid would be back at school, hanging out with his friends. Joey wouldn't even remember Gregory had ever been gone. Kids were resilient, and all of Diana's talk about hurting the boy was just so much psychobabble to mask the heart of the matter.

That night on the boat when he told her, she had made love to him with a ferocity, an abandon he'd never imagined possible. In the darkened room he had stripped his soul bare and revealed his vulnerability, and she hadn't flinched. Not even when he'd told her his chances of fathering a child were remote had her resolve weakened. Her hazel eyes had softened with compassion, but not pity. She'd spoken to him with a touch of fear, but without revulsion. In the heart of the night she had proved him to be more of a man than he had ever dreamed he could be. Diana was a woman of passion and loyalty, a woman able to commit herself to a lifetime with one man.

Unfortunately Gregory wasn't that one man, after all.

She couldn't handle his situation and she'd opted out. He chuckled hollowly. How many times had he wished he could do the same thing? Why was it okay for a woman to walk, and a federal offense for a man to admit he just couldn't cut it?

Men were expected to cherish their woman through PMS and menopause, through sagging breasts and broken dreams. Men were expected to love their women for who they were, not for what they might have been.

If a man truly loved a woman, he was expected to look beyond minor setbacks like sterility, and spin happy tales about successful adoptions; but when the tables were turned, how many women with ticking biological clocks would be able to do the same?

Not many.

And obviously not Diana Travis.

It was human nature to look for an escape hatch, and she'd found hers. He glanced down at the globe on his desk, and his gaze roamed the expanse of blue water called the Caribbean. With a little luck, his escape hatch would be there, waiting for him.

With a lot of luck, it would be enough.

DIANA WAS on the realtor's doorstep by nine the next morning. Ignatius, howling, was once again ensconced in his cat carrier, and she had fed and watered Boris and bidden him a teary farewell as she left Gull Cottage—and a thousand memories—behind.

"A young man and his son are on their way out," said Mrs. Geller's replacement cheerfully. "I know they'll care for Boris as wonderfully as you did."

Handing over the key to Gull Cottage hurt as much as if she'd been handing over her heart.

In a way, that was exactly what she had done. In one month she had handed over her heart to a man she'd once thought perfect, only to discover he wasn't perfect at all.

"That'll teach you," she said aloud as she started up the station wagon and cast a glance at Ignatius in his cat carrier. Maybe Mother knew best when it came to coffee rings and house-itosis, but she sure came in a distant last on affairs of the heart.

She'd get back on schedule, the way she was supposed to be. She'd drop off Ignatius with Paula and Art, then find herself a hotel room somewhere and finish off her manuscript. She'd exercise more and eat less and do her best to pretend her heart wasn't breaking, and when Labor Day rolled around she'd go out there and search for a man who really *was* perfect—not just perfectly beautiful.

She couldn't resist one last drive along Main Street, and to her surprise found herself coming up on the East End Animal Hospital. Mary Ann's car was parked in front, and there was no sign of the Corvette anywhere. Diana signaled a left, then turned into the lot. The least she could do was say goodbye to the woman.

"You're making a mistake," said Mary Ann the moment she saw Diana. "There's still time to make it to the marina before he leaves."

Diana stiffened. "I thought you'd be the first one to understand."

"I *do* understand. That's why I'm telling you to get your butt out there as fast as you can and hold on."

"He's abandoning Joey."

"He has a right, Diana. We don't have any hold over him."

"Well, neither do I. He can sail to hell and back for all I care."

"You're making a mistake."

"I don't think I am. He's a selfish bastard."

"Yes," Mary Ann agreed, "but he's also one of the best friends I've ever had. You don't give that up without a fight."

"He's no friend of mine," Diana snapped.

Mary Ann forced a grin. "I wish I could say the same thing."

"You can have him."

"Don't I wish."

Despite herself, Diana laughed. "Making jokes this early in the morning must be a good sign."

The red-haired woman shrugged her slender shoulders. "It is. Joey's second test results were much better than expected. I have my fingers crossed."

"Will Joey still be having surgery?"

"Friday," said Mary Ann. "That just might do the trick."

There in the middle of her unhappiness a miracle was taking shape, and her joy over Joey stood out in sharp contrast to the pain she felt over losing Gregory. How wonderful to know miracles were still possible! "I'll call you Friday night," said Diana. "I want a full report."

"Why don't you stay at my house?" Mary Ann offered. "I'd like the company."

Diana was deeply touched, but she shook her head. "I don't think so." Memories of Gregory would be too hard to bear on familiar territory. "I'm heading back to New Jersey."

"And they say *I'm* crazy...." She walked Diana back to the station wagon. "Can't get you to change your mind about driving to the marina?"

Diana let the question slide. "Is the birthday party still on for the fourteenth?"

"Sure," said Mary Ann. "You'll come?"

"I wouldn't miss it for the world."

Tears brimmed in Mary Ann's blue eyes as she gave Diana a fierce hug. "Joey's gonna be thrilled."

"No more than I," said Diana. "I wouldn't miss that birthday party for anything on earth."

Not even for the chance to be with the man she loved. Life was too precious, too uncertain a thing to take lightly, and she intended to celebrate Joey's life with the people who loved him most. And if Gregory couldn't find it within his soul to rejoice at this one small victory, then she felt sorrier for him than he would ever know.

You're a selfish SOB, Stewart, she thought, as she headed for the highway and left East Hampton behind.

She must have been a fool to fall in love with a man like that.

AS IT TURNED OUT, Gregory was right about one thing: there was nothing in Diana's bag of homegrown remedies that could heal a broken heart. She hid herself away in a hotel in Somerset, near Paula's home, and managed to finish her book by the beginning of the second week in August.

Suddenly she was left with time to think, and she didn't like the direction those thoughts were ʌking her. She was a creature of habit, the General's daughter, a woman who had gone through her life believing that people and events could be scheduled and compartmentalized like items on a grocery store shelf, only to discover that her heart was the one thing she could not control.

"It doesn't matter," she said to Paula over lunch on August 13. The two women were sitting on Paula's patio, while Kath and Jenny played in a sandbox next to them. "He's probably halfway to Barbados by now, up to his eyeballs in tropical maidens."

"You sound jealous."

"Hah!" Diana speared a leaf of romaine lettuce with her fork. "We're finished. He's ancient history."

Paula's earthy rejoinder stopped Diana cold.

"I can't believe you said that!" Paula had always been annoyingly pure of speech.

"I'll say a lot more than that, if you don't come clean."

Diana dropped her fork to the china plate with a clatter.

"What do you want from me, Paulie? Do you want me to fall weeping at your feet?"

"I'd settle for some frank talk."

"He's gone and I'm still here. That's about all there is to say."

"You really *are* just like Dad: arrogant, argumentative and too damned pigheaded for your own good. If you weren't so heartbroken, I'd almost say it served you right."

"Would you mind speaking English?"

"Gregory," Paula said, leaning forward in her rattan chair. "You shouldn't have let him go."

"Mind your own business, Paula."

"I have been," her sister shot back, "and see where it's gotten you? You're heartbroken."

"I'll live."

"Sure you will—you'll live the life of a miserable old maid." Paula grinned. "Not that you don't deserve it, mind you, but you'd probably end up living with me, and I don't think I could stand it."

"Very funny." Diana redirected her attention to her Cobb Salad. "Only a fool would sail to the Caribbean during hurricane season."

"Only a fool would let him go."

Diana addressed her salad with renewed enthusiasm.

"You were like this as a kid," Paula observed. "Whenever things didn't go your own way, you picked up your Barbie doll and went home. Well, this time you're not going to get away with it."

"Of course I won't," said Diana evenly. "At the moment I don't have a home to go to."

Paula looked as if she'd like to leap across the table and strangle her younger sister, Diana thought. What was restraining her?

"What is it you want, Diana? I thought you finally understood that you can't have everything—none of us can."

"*You* have everything," Diana said, gesturing toward the

house and swimming pool and landscaped property. "A husband. Two kids. A home in the suburbs—"

"You're right," said Paula with a visibly sheepish smile. "I *do* have everything, but if you think I didn't have to compromise in order to get the happiness I have, then you're a bigger fool than I thought."

"You don't understand," Diana said, burying her face in her hands. "He isn't the man I thought he was."

"No man could be what you thought Gregory was. You were looking for a saint. What you found was a human being."

"Don't go getting philosophical on me," Diana warned through her sniffles. "That's my territory." She told her sister about Joey, and about Gregory's refusal to stand by the boy. "How could I be so wrong about someone? He's selfish and—"

"Scared."

Diana looked up at her sister. "What?"

"He's scared, Di. Don't tell me you didn't realize that."

"He's not afraid of anything, Paulie. The man believes he's invulnerable."

"You'd better turn in your notepad, Mother, because you missed the mark this time. He's not running away from Joey. He's running for his life."

"You don't know Gregory. You can't possibly understand."

"I know you're too much in love to see clearly. I know you're hurt and tired, and afraid you're going to regret what you gave up if you commit yourself to him."

"You're wrong, Paulie." Diana heard her voice crack with emotion. "I'm not."

"Think about it," her sister ordered gently. "You can lie to me, but don't lie to yourself." She gestured toward her curly-haired daughters playing in the sunshine. "That's a big sacrifice, kiddo. Do you think you can do it?"

Diana's heart ached with love for the two little girls, who had become such an important part of her life, and she wondered if her maternal instinct was destined to be channeled into being the world's best aunt.

"Before I met Gregory, I would have said no, but now—" She hesitated, uncertain how to put such complex feelings into words. For two weeks she had wrestled with the question, and each time she had come up with the same answer. She loved him. She could no longer imagine life without him.

"Yes," she said at last. *And it wouldn't be a sacrifice. Not really.* If only she had realized that before she left East Hampton, things might have been different. In her heart she had always known that a man would be at the center of her happiness, that a solid marriage would be the foundation upon which everything else was built.

"Don't go banking on miracles," Paula warned. "You'll only get hurt that way."

"The only miracle is that we found each other in the first place." *Only a fool would turn away.*

"You may never get pregnant, Di."

"I know. I'm willing to take the chance." She laughed hollowly. "Not that the man in question is around anymore to volunteer."

"Did you talk about adoption?"

"We didn't have time." Her voice was husky as unshed tears battled for release. "We didn't have time for very much at all." *Only to fall in love and dream of a future we'll never have.* "I was a coward, Paulie. I couldn't face the uncertainty," *Or the blunt truth, until now.* She'd created the perfect man in her mind, and cast Gregory Stewart in that role. When the perfect man turned out to be mortal, she no longer knew what to do with her dream. Gregory hadn't been the only one to turn and run; Diana saw that now. She had run as fast as she could away from reality, only to find that no fantasy of the perfect man could possibly compete with the reality of Gregory Stewart.

The man she loved. In sickness and in health. With children or without. Forever and beyond.

"And—?" Paula prompted.

"And what difference does it make? He's gone, and I'm here, and none of it really matters, after all."

Paula fixed Diana with one of her best big-sister looks. "If you can handle his situation the way it is, then track him down. If you can't—" Her sister shrugged eloquently. "Well, if you can't, then you'll be ready to start looking on Labor Day, right on schedule." Paula's smile was rueful now. "Only you can have a whirlwind romance and a broken heart and not lose a day into the bargain."

Only me, thought Diana as she bent down to hug her nieces. Her tears fell onto their soft curls and sparkled in the sunshine. Even if she wanted to run to Gregory, she couldn't, because he was out there in the middle of the ocean, alone and out of reach, just the way he'd wanted to be.

How I spent my summer vacation....

What a column that would make.

What a colossal joke.

Chapter Nineteen

The Marino house was filled to the rafters. Relatives jammed the doorways, roamed the scruffy backyard and littered the porch and patio with cake crumbs and cigarette butts and good cheer. And why not? Joey had come through his surgery with flying colors, and was home for his birthday with a prognosis for a future as bright as the red, white and blue balloons that bobbed happily everywhere Diana looked.

Apparently there would be at least one happy ending that summer, and Diana rejoiced for Joey and Mary Ann and their victory. If only her own story had a happy ending, as well....

Like a fool, she had hoped against hope that Gregory would be part of the celebration. During the long drive out to Quogue she had imagined, time and again, how he would look, what she would say, how it would feel to see him come through the doorway and be swept up into his arms, the way she had been so many times before.

She forced a smile as Joey's Aunt Ida and Uncle Joe took the floor, to show the youngster what dancing was all about. She'd met so many people that afternoon, aunts and uncles, grandmothers and grandfathers, friends and acquaintances who'd all found the time to drop by and offer the boy a piece of their own strength. Dave and Peggy were there with the baby—how big he'd gotten so quickly!—and even Charlie had raced by to drop off a present for Joey and some toys for Daisy and her pups, who showed little sign of leaving the comfort of the Marino abode.

To think that the one man who understood the true nature of Joey's triumph hadn't bothered to even call....

Tears were coming all too easily these days, and she blinked rapidly to clear her eyes, then slipped out the back door to regain her composure. Discovering that Mary Ann Marino had slipped out right after her, Diana wandered over with Joey's mother toward the swing set in the far corner of the yard.

Mary Ann lit a cigarette and sat down on a swing. "Have you heard from him?" she asked.

Diana shook her head. "Have you?"

"Not a word. I thought he'd at least manage a card for Joey."

"So did I," Diana said. "I guess there aren't any mailboxes on the high seas."

Laughter rang out from the small house, and the two women listened to Joey's high-pitched voice as he exclaimed over one of his presents.

"Joey loved that videotape on the Yankees you gave him," said Mary Ann, flicking ash from her cigarette. It was the first time since Diana had known the woman that Mary Ann's smile actually reached her eyes. "He wants to stay up late tonight and watch the whole thing."

Diana made some pleasant, innocuous remark that died out a few words before the end of the sentence. *What am I doing here?* she asked herself. *These are Gregory's friends, not mine.* She must look like some pathetic, homeless fool, clinging to the remnants of a relationship that hadn't lasted.

She glanced at her watch and looked down at Mary Ann. "I'd better get going. I have a long drive back to my sister's."

"You can spend the night," Mary Ann offered. "I can't offer you your own suite, but I can give you clean sheets and the best pillow in the house."

Diana shook her head. "Deadlines are calling me," she

said, hoping God would forgive her the ubiquitous social lie. "I should leave."

They went inside, where Diana quickly said her goodbyes. Joey was the center of attention, surrounded by a pile of gaily wrapped presents that almost reached the ceiling. He was still thin, but his cheeks had filled out and his color was rosy. For the first time it looked as if the boy actually had a future to plan. Diana's heart filled with a joy so sweet that it stole her breath away. She prayed that by this time next year he would be taller and stronger, healthy and happy—God willing, she prayed Joey would be just an everyday teenage boy. What a wonderful wish.

"Are we still invited to the twins' birthday party in October?" Joey asked, blushing at the bear hug she gave him.

"Joey!" his mother warned with an apologetic look at Diana. "Don't—"

"Of course, you're still invited," Diana said. "October 28. Paula will send you the invitations in a few weeks."

Cars filled the driveway and cluttered the street. Her own rented Buick was halfway down the block, wedged in between a Caddy and a beat-up Volkswagen with Connecticut plates. No sign of a vintage, black Corvette.

"Get used to it," she muttered as she walked slowly down the quiet, residential street. He was gone, exactly as he'd said he would be, and it was high time she got her act together and accepted the fact that it was over.

A wolf whistle sounded from somewhere behind her, and she ignored it. The only good thing about heartbreak was the weight loss that came with it. *Too bad, Stewart,* she thought, *I finally have decent thighs, and you're not around to see them.* Wasn't that just the way of the world?

She stopped next to the driver's door of the Buick and was about to insert the key, when she heard a car slowing down behind her. Teenagers, she thought. That was what she got for wearing a mini. She should turn around and give them a good look at her thirty-five-year-old face. That would teach them to go cruising.

"Diana."

Her hand shook, and she struggled to turn the key in the lock. *It's my imagination.... I was sitting in the sun too long.... I haven't slept well lately.... I haven't eaten....* It simply couldn't be him.

"What happened to the station wagon?"

The key fell to the ground, and she rested her head on the roof of the car, suddenly feeling dizzy and weak. This was carrying imagination too far.

But then she felt an arm snake around her waist, and the scent of salt air and soap blossomed around her as she turned and saw Gregory Stewart.

"I knew I'd find you here." He looked nervous and hopeful and painfully vulnerable.

She swallowed hard against a violent swelling of emotion. "I never thought I'd find *you* here."

"There's one thing to be said for heading out to sea alone: you have plenty of time to think."

Her chest ached from the rapid pounding of her heart. "Any conclusions?"

"You were right," he said. "I owe this to Joey."

"And yourself?"

He drew her closer. "And myself."

"I've done a lot of thinking, as well," she said, aware that each word she spoke carried the importance of a lifetime. "You were right, too, Gregory. I *was* scared. I didn't know if I was ready to take a chance on you. I never thought I'd have to compromise."

"And now?"

Why not go for broke? "Living without you isn't living at all. I can't imagine anything sweeter than to go through life loving you," she said. "That's more than most people get." Good friends, a career she loved, and a man who was more wonderful than any she'd ever dreamed about. And if somehow that happiness could include a child for them to love, then all the better. But the answer to that question was beyond her grasp, for now.

"I want children." The pain of that admission was visible in his eyes, and she ached for what it had cost him to show himself vulnerable. "I want children with you."

Tears welled in her eyes. "Having your baby would be the most wonderful thing in the world," she whispered. "But even if it never happens, I'll still be the happiest woman in the world."

"There's still a possibility," he said, opening his soul to her.

"We'll just have to keep trying, won't we?"

"Every chance we get." He smiled and the old sparkle was back. "I'm not against adoption."

Her heart soared. "Neither am I."

"I've spent five years running from the truth," he said, brushing a stray curl back from her face. "I had cancer and I beat it, and I've felt guilty ever since. That damned all-clear mark became a badge of honor." He stopped and she could feel his heart beating faster beneath her hand. "When Joey got sick, I couldn't handle it. I couldn't figure why I beat it, and a good kid like that had to pay."

"That's not the way life works, Gregory." She couldn't wait to see his face when he heard Joey's good news.

"I know that now." No one had a guarantee of happiness. You had to work for it every day, for the rest of your life— no matter how long or short that life might be. Cancer had little to do with it; courage, everything. "I've changed," he said, meeting her eyes, "but one thing hasn't: I still love you."

She didn't bother to hide her tears. "We have a lot to work out." She wrapped her arms about his waist and felt his warmth and weight against her.

"Let's start with your great husband hunt." He kissed her mouth and throat and shoulder. "It's finished."

"Are you sure?"

"Positive. You're going to marry me."

"I love it when you're macho."

His grin was wicked and wonderful. "Just wait until the wedding night."

"I might not be able to."

"That's what I was hoping you'd say."

"We still have a lot to learn about each other," she warned.

"We'll have a lifetime to do it."

"What about your trip to the Caribbean?"

"How does a sailing honeymoon sound? We could get married on Saturday and leave the next morning."

She tried to speak, but her throat was so tight that the words couldn't escape.

"This time all the cards will be on the table," he said. "I love you, Diana. I always will."

She rose on tiptoe and whispered something into his ear, something private and warm and filled with promise for the future, and then she surrendered herself to the power and wonder of love.

Arm in arm, they went back into the house to wish Joey a happy birthday.

At long last, they really did have it all.

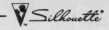

SPECIAL EDITION™

COMING IN JUNE

HER LAST
FIRST DATE

by *USA TODAY* bestsellling author
SUSAN MALLERY

After one too many bad dates, Crissy Phillips
finally swore off men. Recently widowed,
pediatrician Josh Daniels can't risk losing his
heart. With an intense attraction pulling them
together, will their fear keep them apart?
Or will one wild night change everything...?

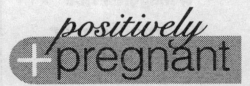

*Sometimes the unexpected
is the best news of all....*

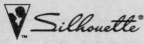

LIKE MOTHER, LIKE DAUGHTER (But In a Good Way)

with stories by
Jennifer Greene,
Nancy Robards Thompson
and Peggy Webb

Don't miss these three unforgettable stories about the unbreakable—and sometimes infuriating—bonds between mothers and daughters and the men who get caught in the madness (when they're not causing it!).

HARLEQUIN
Next

HARLEQUIN®

Mediterranean NIGHTS™

Tycoon Elias Stamos is launching his newest luxury cruise ship from his home port in Greece. But someone from his past is eager to expose old secrets and to see the Stamos empire crumble.

Mediterranean Nights
launches in June 2007 with...

FROM RUSSIA, WITH LOVE
by *Ingrid Weaver*

Join the guests and crew of *Alexandra's Dream* as they are drawn into a world of glamour, romance and intrigue in this new 12-book series.